I've Got
a Secret

CANDY APPLE BOOKS...
JUST FOR YOU.
SWEET. FRESH. FUN.
TAKE A BITE!

The Accidental Cheerleader
by Mimi McCoy

The Boy Next Door
by Laura Dower

Miss Popularity
by Francesco Sedita

How to Be a Girly Girl in Just Ten Days
by Lisa Papademetriou

Drama Queen
by Lara Bergen

The Babysitting Wars
by Mimi McCoy

Totally Crushed
by Eliza Willard

I've Got a Secret

by LARA BERGEN

SCHOLASTIC INC.

New York Toronto London Auckland Sydney
Mexico City New Delhi Hong Kong Buenos Aires

For Kitty

ISBN-13: 978-0-545-03427-2
ISBN-10: 0-545-03427-2

Copyright © 2008 by Lara Bergen

12 11 10 9 8 7   9 10 11 12 13/0
Printed in the U.S.A.   40
First printing, January 2008

Chapter One

From: AllieOop@cablewest.com
To: Hays3@amerimail.com
Sent: Saturday, July 21, 2007 5:54 PM
Subject: MISS YOU!
Attach: BEST FRIENDS 101.jpg

Hey, Mandy girl! Just got home and I am SO sad! :-(
I miss camp SO much! :,(Don't you?! I wish it
could last forever – real life is so boring! Or – as
camp director Bill-Take-a-Chill-Pill would
say – "This is not – I say NOT – acceptable!"

    Of course, I know you're happy to be back with
you-know-who! Lucky dog! Please – you have to write
me back and tell me all about your big reunion!
YBFF (Your best friend forever!),
Allie

OBTW – I played our talent show DVD for my brother on the ride home, and guess what he said? Give up? "That girl who played those dudes in your skit was SO awesome!" You're such a star! :-)
OBTW2 – Remember this picture?

Amanda laughed out loud as she scrolled down to a picture of her and another girl. They stood arm in arm, both wearing messy wigs and goofy, clown-like grins. She shook her head and was about to hit REPLY when Kate, her oldest friend, appeared in the doorway.

"Amanda!" Kate called out, running in with a wide grin on her freckled face. "I missed you so much! How was camp? You look so tan!"

Amanda jumped up and happily hugged her friend.

"You look tan, too!" she said, standing back after a moment. "I thought it rained a lot in Ireland."

"It *does*," said Kate. "Believe me! There was literally moss growing on my shoes." She smiled and turned her head from side to side. "This is from my sister's self-tanner. I snuck a little this morning. Not too orange?"

Amanda nodded her approval. "No, it's good. But you missed a spot, right there." She pointed to

2

Kate's neck and giggled as her friend quickly tucked in her chin.

"I'll have to get that later," said Kate. Then she laughed and grabbed Amanda's hand. "Right now, I want to hear all about camp. Oh!" She reached into her pocket. "But first, I brought you this!"

She pulled out a small green box and handed it to Amanda, who opened it at once. Inside was a silver ring with two hands holding a heart and a crown on top. It was one of the prettiest things Amanda had ever seen!

"It's a claddagh ring," Kate told her. "I got it in the village where my grandma grew up. It *can* be a symbol of love," she explained, "with the hands and the heart and all. But lots of people wear them as friendship rings, too. Do you like it?"

"I love it!" said Amanda, slipping the ring on and admiring how it looked on her hand. "Thanks so much!"

"Wait," Kate told her, grinning. "You've got to wear it like this." She took the ring from Amanda's finger and turned it upside down. "This way, heart out, means you're available; your heart is open." She worked her eyebrows up and down. "The other way, heart in, means someone's already captured your heart. And we don't want anyone thinking you're not available, now, do we?"

Amanda laughed — weakly. *If Kate only knew!* And that's when she almost, *almost* spilled her summer secret. But she couldn't.

Guess what, Kate? There are *some people who think I'm unavailable. A whole* camp *full of people, in fact! How crazy is that? What made them think that? Funny you should ask. Turns out, I lied and said I had a boyfriend. No, really. I did!*

Of course, Amanda hadn't *meant* to lie. It just kind of . . . happened.

"Okay!" said Kate, plopping down on Amanda's desk chair. "I'm ready. What was camp like? How were the counselors? Did you make any friends?"

Amanda took a deep breath and tried to think about where to begin.

Of course Kate would want to know everything about camp. After all, it had been her idea to go to the summer arts camp in the first place! (Camp was a loose term, since it was held on the campus of a tiny all-girl college — without a single tent or cabin or canoe for miles around!) They signed up to go *together,* of course, like everything they'd done since first grade.

It was all planned out: Amanda would play her cello, and Kate would play her flute. By the end of camp, they'd both be good enough to make first chair in orchestra in the fall. *Not the most exciting*

4

summer, Amanda thought, *but way better than baby-sitting Kate's little brother and sister at the pool, like last year.*

This perfect plan, however, was not meant to be. Instead of spending three carefree weeks rooming with Amanda and becoming an expert at playing her flute, Kate had been whisked off to Ireland with the rest of her family. Her grandmother was turning seventy-five, and had decided the whole gang should help her celebrate in the tiny town where she was born.

And Amanda? Well, Amanda ended up making a million new friends, not touching her cello once, and having the absolute best summer ever (despite one massive, ridiculous, totally *accidental* lie).

None of which she was prepared to admit to Kate.

"So," Kate teased. "I'm *waiting*. And what were you reading that was so funny when I came in?"

"What?" Amanda watched as Kate turned to face the blinking computer screen. "Oh . . . uh . . . nothing," she said quickly. "Just an e-mail from someone at camp."

"*Really*?" said Kate. "Who? A *boy*?"

Amanda almost laughed at the absurdity of the idea — then caught her breath as she realized that her friend was *reading* the e-mail.

"Wow . . . you made a good friend," Kate said slowly. Her tone was somewhat less than thrilled.

"Oh, well, you know . . ." Amanda shrugged, not sure why she felt so guilty.

"And her name's Allie?" Kate went on.

"Yeah," said Amanda. She tried, unsuccessfully, to lean between Kate and the computer screen. "She was my roommate. They had to put someone else in, you know . . . when you couldn't go."

Kate nodded and frowned very, very slightly. "And she calls you '*Mandy*'?"

Amanda shrugged again. "She just started calling me that . . . she likes nicknames, I guess. I don't know." Amanda hadn't minded the name, though no one had ever called her Mandy before. "Do you like it?" she asked Kate.

Kate thought it over for a moment. "It's cute." She grinned. "But it sounds like someone else. What's Allie like?" she asked, switching gears.

"She's . . . uh . . . really nice." Amanda smiled, but took extra care not to sound too enthusiastic. "She's from upstate, and going into seventh grade, too. She's really into comedy and drama and stuff like that. She's the one who talked me into trying out for the improv group."

"Improv group?" asked Kate, confused. "But what about the cello?"

6

Amanda's eyes grew wide. "Well . . . my bridge broke." She paused.

"Yeah?" Kate urged. "And you couldn't get it fixed?"

Amanda shrugged.

"Are you kidding?" said Kate in half sincere, half mock disbelief. "So you didn't play it for three whole weeks?"

Amanda wrinkled her nose and guiltily shook her head.

Kate twirled a copper curl around her finger and grinned. "Well, at least you won't be playing circles around me in orchestra," she joked. "But that was the whole point of camp! Your *bridge*?" She laughed. "Come on — you so totally could have fixed that!"

Amanda maintained her innocence for one more second, then burst into giggles. "Maybe," she said. "But that's between you and me and my cello. Understand?"

"Oh, I understand," said Kate, still smiling.

But does she? Amanda wondered. Kate loved music so much. Amanda doubted she could ever be tempted to leave it for one week, let alone three! But for Amanda, it had been as easy as opening her cello case that first day of camp and seeing the helpless, dangling strings and the crumbled plane of wood that had supported them.

She had just met her roommate, Allie, five minutes before, and she could remember the whole scene in their dorm room like it was yesterday:

"You know what you should do, Mandy?" Allie had asked.

"What?" asked Amanda, once she finally realized that Mandy meant *her*. "Call 1-800-FIX-MY-CELLO?"

Allie laughed. "Very funny. No, what you should do is switch your arts elective to improv — with me!"

Amanda looked down at her poor cello — the same one she'd practiced on every day since third grade — and bit her lip. "What's improv?" she asked.

"Oh, it's *so* great!" said Allie. She put down the brush she'd been trying to tug through her curly hair and rummaged around in the pink duffel bag on her bed. "At least, I hope it will be." She pulled out a huge pack of bubble gum. "It's short for 'improvisational theater' — you know, where you make up skits on the spot. Like that show, *Whose Line Is It Anyway?*" She unwrapped a thick, pink wad of gum and popped it in her mouth, then offered a piece to Amanda. "I mon, dot show ishn't *always* fohnny, bot . . ."

8

"Thanks," Amanda said, accepting the gum with a curious smile. "But I don't think I've seen it."

"Doesn't matter." Allie shrugged and chewed away happily. "The improv class should be hilarious. And how fun would that be — to be roommates *and* do improv together?"

Amanda worked the gum, letting the minty flavor fill her throat. "I don't know. The cello's what I'm here for — it's how I talked my parents into letting me come. I mean, I'm no Yo-Yo Ma, but it's kind of what I *do*."

The bubble Allie was working on fell flat across her chin. "Yo-Yo *who*?" she asked. Then she frowned as she freed a string of gum from a chunk of her sunbleached hair.

Amanda laughed. "He's a great cellist — someone my mom is always telling me to aspire to." She put a hand on one hip and raised an admonishing eyebrow. " '*Amanda!* Do you *really* think Yo-Yo Ma's mother let him go to a movie when he had a concert the next day? And a PG-13 movie at that! Dear, it just wouldn't be *responsible!* ' "

Allie fell back on her bed in a fit of laughter. "Oh my gosh!" she howled. "Your mom sounds worse than mine!"

"If you only knew," Amanda told her, grinning.

"Well, I get it," said Allie. "The improv would

just be *so* much fun." She sat up and chomped her gum noisily, thinking for a moment. "And don't you think your mom would be kind of psyched to find out you spent your summer trying something *different*? Maybe finding something *else* you were really good at?"

"Absolutely not!" said Amanda immediately. Then she smiled. No, she couldn't see her mom being psyched to find that out — not after forking over as much for three weeks of intense cello instruction as she and Amanda's dad usually spent on lessons for the whole year. As for Amanda herself, *she* just might be able to see how it would be fun. . . .

"I guess," she said slowly, "it wouldn't hurt to ask the camp director. And you know," she went on, as the idea took root in her brain, "without my friend, Kate, here, orchestra really wouldn't be half as much fun."

"Totally!" said Allie. "We'd have a much better time together!"

Amanda blew a bubble to match the one Allie was working on, and reached out to close the lid on her sorry-looking cello.

"Ugh," she groaned, sucking the gum in with a sudden, sodden *snap*. "I feel kind of like I did when we put our dog to sleep last summer."

Allie gave the case a gentle pat. "Don't worry, old cello, old pal. You're just going to sleep for a little while. When you wake up, everything will be just as it was before."

And, basically, Allie was right. . . .

Amanda's mom had seen to it that her cello was repaired the *minute* she got home. Her dad had helped carry in her bags, then handed her a list of three weeks' worth of waiting chores. And Kate had come over to catch up on everything.

And yet, things weren't *exactly* the same. Amanda had a secret — something she'd never had from Kate before.

She could remember, just as clearly, how *that* had happened, too. It was on the very first night of camp, just before lights out, when all the girls in her hall had come over to Amanda and Allie's room to hang out and talk about the boys. Once that topic had been covered, Allie (who just naturally seemed to assume the role of the Life of Every Party) had brought out pictures of her family and friends from home to show. Amanda had realized that she, too, had pictures with her, and laid them out for all to see.

"These are my parents," she'd said, pointing to a smiling couple. "That," she explained, "is my dad's official picture smile — even though I always tell

11

him he looks like a dork — and that's my mom's official pose. She says it makes her legs look thinner. I say it makes her look like she has to pee."

Allie and the others laughed, and Amanda happily went on.

She held up another picture. "This is me and my best friend, Kate," she said. "She would have been here, if it weren't for her grandmother. . . . Anyway, this is us on spring break. Her parents took us to Florida. You wouldn't know it, 'cause we're wearing towels, but Kate's wearing this two-piece her mom bought her. She didn't know it till she got it wet, but the bottom was so big, it totally fell off every time she got hit by a wave. She was mortified, of course! So we had to go get her a new one after the first day there."

"Oh no!" Allie squealed, laughing and reaching for another photo. "And who, may I ask, is *this*?"

"Ooh!" another girl, Anna, chimed in. "He's cute!"

"Is that Mandy's boyfriend?" asked another. "Let me see!"

"Huh?" said Amanda. "Who?" She looked down at the picture from the previous spring's sixth grade trip. Taking the whole sixth grade to Adventure Park at the end of the year was a middle school tradition. And though no school function was without its torturous moments, she and Kate had had a pretty great time. The only strict rule was that you stick with a buddy at all times.

Of course, there were two tiny problems: Amanda loved roller coasters, and Kate did not; Kate loved rides that spun, and Amanda did not. So they compromised. Kate stood in line with Amanda and waited on the platform while she rode the roller coasters, and Amanda did the same with Kate on the spinning rides. It wasn't a perfect plan — but it worked.

The picture Allie had zeroed in on had been taken on Dead Man's Curve, when Amanda had found herself sitting next to a boy she knew vaguely from school. Sean? Or Ron? Or John? Something like that. He'd been with a big, odd-numbered group, and when it came time to board the ride, he'd wound up in the front row with Amanda. She couldn't remember if they'd actually spoken. Knowing her, she probably went over a million charming pleasantries in her head and ended up saying nothing. But at the end of the ride, she'd seen this picture (taken halfway down the first big drop) for sale and Kate had talked her into getting it, saying that she looked like a model. Amanda, truth be told, had a hard time seeing past the giant, gaping O her mouth was forming — but good pictures were hard to come by.

As for the surprisingly serene-looking boy sitting beside her on the ride, she honestly hadn't given him much thought.

"So, Mandy, tell us about your *boyfriend*!" Allie cooed.

"Boyfriend?" Amanda echoed.

"Yeah! He *is* your boyfriend, right?"

Amanda looked at her new friend's face — and all the others — so eager. They reminded her of those geese at the park that just kept coming, long after she'd run out of crumbs, till she finally had no other choice but to run away like a maniac, screaming. (Didn't that happen to everyone?)

Then she looked at her photo-mate a little more closely. He wasn't exactly the prince she'd have dreamed up for herself, but he certainly wasn't bad, either.

Maybe she had more crumbs to toss out than she thought.

"Uh . . . yeah . . . yeah, right," she stammered.

There. She'd said it. And the rest came pretty easily. For the next three weeks, she was Mandy — of "John and Mandy." (That *was* his name, she was sure of it.) Mandy and John. John and Mandy. Sitting in a tree . . . and all of that.

Of course, it made liking any boy at camp

impossible. But it sure made her popular with the other girls!

It was weird, though — and not just the part about having an imaginary boyfriend. It was also weird how carried away people's imaginations could get!

"Hey! Is this guitar pick *John's*?" Allie had asked when she'd spotted an old pick on Amanda's nightstand. "Does he play in a band or something?"

"Uh . . . sure," said Amanda.

(Why bother to say she'd found it in the parking lot the day her parents dropped her off? Talk about unexciting.)

And, "Why do you have July seventh circled on your calendar?" another girl, Tallulah, had asked one day. "Is it *John's* birthday? Is he already thirteen?"

"Uh . . . sure," Amanda had replied.

(Why say it was really her father's birthday? After all, it was also Ringo Starr's . . . as her dad liked to remind her. It *could* have been John's, too.)

"He's a Cancer!" noted Allie from across the room. "That is *so* totally good!"

And then, of course, there were the questions about all the unsigned "I'll miss you" and "Have fun" notes in her bags and cello case.

How could she possibly tell Allie and everyone else they were from her best *girl*friend Kate — who'd helped her pack? They all so naturally assumed the notes were from John, aka the greatest *boy*friend in the whole, entire world.

There was no way at all.

By the end of the three weeks, everyone thought Amanda was the luckiest girl in the world. To tell the truth, she *did* feel lucky. But not because she had an awesome boyfriend. She felt lucky to have ended up being roommates with Allie. Everything with her was just so . . . *easy*.

It wasn't that Amanda didn't *want* to make friends, but she never knew what to say. And maybe she wasn't the only girl to ever feel that way, but it sure seemed like it sometimes. This, however, was definitely *not* the case for Allie.

Allie could talk to anyone, it seemed, and leave them begging for more. She was always smiling, always friendly, always making people feel like they were lucky to be around her. From the first day of camp, people swarmed around her like ants at a great big, honey-covered picnic. At meals, kids invited Allie to sit with them. At improv, they asked her to do skits with them. At free time, they asked her to play hearts or volleyball or badminton with them. At night, they asked her to share their junk food and play truth or dare with them.

And the crazy, amazing thing was that because Amanda was her roommate and because Allie seemed to truly like her, Amanda was getting all the attention, too. Never, ever had she felt so at the center of it all. And she didn't have to act any differently or put on any kind of show. All she had to do was bask in Allie's glow.

Amanda had even thought up the skit she and Allie did for the camp's talent show finale. It was just a two-person show, but in it they portrayed six different camp counselors, plus the camp's *energetic* director (Bill "Take-a-Chill-Pill" McGill, as Allie called him), who they made the emcee. It was a counselor beauty contest, complete with a question-and-answer round and a talent competition. The skit won them not just first place, but a standing ovation, too.

Of course, Amanda had always loved music, but she found she didn't miss it. Not the littlest bit. This other side of her was having too much fun to care about the cello.

Truly, she'd dreaded the end of camp. And now, home for just four hours, she already missed the energy, the camaraderie, the laughs. And she already hated not being able to share it all with

Kate. She'd never had a secret from Kate before. She'd never had to. Any secrets she did have were Kate's secrets, too.

But how do you tell someone who's known you forever that, for three weeks, you've done things and acted ways you never have before? How do you tell someone who respects you that, for three weeks, you let a dorm full of people believe a big, fat lie? And how do you tell your very best friend in the world that, for three weeks, you had *another* best friend who's *completely* different from her?

As far as Amanda was concerned, you couldn't.

"So . . ." said Kate, who'd gone back to reading Amanda's computer screen. "Did all the kids at camp call you 'Mandy'? And who," she went on, "is 'you-know-who,' exactly?"

Click. Amanda reached out and closed the e-mail window with the mouse.

"Forget about that," Amanda said, trying to act cheerful. "I'm dying to hear more about the Old Country. Did you meet a lot of cousins?"

"*Did* I," answered Kate. "The place is crawling with them." She laughed. "Too bad I forgot to bring my camera to your house. . . ."

"We could go back to your house and get it," suggested Amanda. She linked her arm in Kate's.

18

"Okay," Kate agreed. "But then I want to hear about camp and Allie and everyone. By the way . . ." she paused. "Do you want me to start calling you 'Mandy'?"

Amanda thought for a moment, and shrugged. "It was fun at camp. But I guess back at home, Amanda suits me just fine."

"Totally up to you," said Kate, grinning. "If you change your mind, let me know."

Chapter Two

From: AllieOop@cablewest.com
To: Hays3@amerimail.com
Sent: Wednesday, August 1, 2007 7:29 PM
Subject: GUESS WHAT!

No! Don't even try! It's too amazing! Are you
ready? Are you sitting down? Listen to this: My
dad just got transferred to . . . guess where? Your
town!!!!!! :-D No lie! When my parents first told
me, I totally wanted to cry. :,(But when I found
out where we were moving, I thought it must be a
sign! We really were meant to be BFFs! So we're
moving at the end of the month — just before school
starts. I'll send more details later!
YBFF,
Allie

OBTW—When you tell cute BF John, ask him if he has any equally cute friends he might like to set me up with. (Only ½ kidding!)

Amanda stared at the screen, her mouth gaping open. She read the note again. And again. And — just to be sure — again. It definitely said what she thought it said the first time. Allie was moving. Here!

Approximately a thousand and one emotions filled her all at once. She loved Allie! She couldn't wait to hang out with her again, to show her where she lived and where she went to school. And to go to school together and . . .

Wait. There was one huge, enormous, obscenely gigantic problem. Allie was expecting Amanda to have an awesome boyfriend! And not only did Amanda *not* have a boyfriend, she was pretty sure that the boy she'd claimed as her boyfriend didn't even know her name.

What was she going to do when Allie moved here and discovered in exactly two seconds that Amanda was a BFGL — a big, fat, ginormous *liar*?

It had been different at camp. No one had known her. No one had spent six hours a day with her for seven years. No one had already labeled her as a smart, quiet orchestra girl who always turned her

21

work in on time. At camp, they had all come together and Amanda had found herself in a place she'd never been in school.

Not that she was unhappy at school. She had the world's best best friend, after all, and other friends, too. Amanda had no problem with her nice, quiet existence. To tell the truth, she was pretty busy with her homework and music. And when she did have some free time, she usually filled it quite nicely with Kate.

But now Allie was entering the equation — and Amanda just couldn't see how the numbers would add up. Like oil and water, no matter how hard you shook them, real life and Allie were never going to mix. And what if Kate and Allie didn't get along?

So how could she ever choose between them?

Wait! Who was she kidding? Like Allie was even going to talk to Amanda once she discovered her lie.

Lying was bad enough, but what made it even worse was that it was something that, Amanda knew, Allie would never, ever do. And because of this, Allie would never, ever understand it. Maybe she'd be nice enough to forgive Amanda for the crime, but she'd never forget it. And Amanda would never get to bask in Allie's friendship again.

It was brutally clear: Seventh grade was going to be the WORST YEAR EVER — unless Amanda could figure out some way to save it.

She turned off her computer and went to bed, knowing there was little chance she would sleep.

By morning, though, she had the smallest germ of a plan. . . .

"Dad?" Amanda said, sitting down to breakfast in the kitchen and trying to appear casual. "Have you ever thought about asking for a transfer?"

"A transfer?" her father repeated, looking up from his cup of coffee.

"Yeah," said Amanda. She nonchalantly reached for the Cheerios. "You know, moving jobs? Changing cities? Or . . . states?" She tilted the cereal box and concentrated unusually hard on getting the O's into her bowl.

"No, Amanda, I don't think so," her dad said with a dismissive snort.

"Well, have you ever *asked*?" said Amanda, a little more desperately than she'd planned. She kept her eyes on her cereal, though she could feel her parents' stares.

"And who, exactly, am I going to ask?" her dad responded, now setting down his mug and sounding more serious. "It's *my* shoe store. It's been in our family for generations. In the same spot, exactly."

"Well, that's just it," said Amanda. She was careful not to look at her dad, scanning the table in search of the milk instead. "It's high time to move, don't you think? Set down new roots? People need shoes in other parts of the world, too. Shoe stores open other branches, don't they? It's a sign of a successful business." Finally, she looked up into her parents' bewildered faces. "Um . . . could you pass the milk please, Mom?"

"What *is* she talking about?" her dad asked, rubbing his nights' worth of gray-black stubble.

Amanda's mom just shook her head and slid the milk across the table. "I have no idea," she said, shrugging.

Amanda took the milk and let a tiny trickle drip into her bowl. Why waste it now that her appetite was gone?

"Oh! Speaking of moving things," her mom went on, "I almost forgot to tell you, Amanda. Your cello lesson was moved up to ten o'clock. So no lounging around this morning, understand? Yesterday, you were in your pajamas until after lunch." She smiled and raised one eyebrow. "I doubt Yo-Yo Ma's mother let him get away with that."

Amanda stared at the tiny image reflected in her spoon and shook her head. "No, probably not."

Later that morning, Amanda slouched in the passenger's seat of the car as her mom drove to the music school.

"Hey, look!" her mom said, breaking for a stop sign. "The Milners sold their house. It's such a shame they're moving."

Amanda looked up to see the big red SOLD plastered across her neighbors' shiny FOR SALE sign.

Lucky Lucy Milner, she thought to herself, *getting to start over somewhere fresh.* Not that Lucy needed to start over. She had been, by far, one of the more popular girls in school. At the end of the year, the whole class had thrown her a going-away party. Everyone had signed a big banner saying how much they all would miss her. When Lucy got it, she cried like crazy, then went around and hugged every single person — including Amanda — telling them each that she would never forget them, ever. She'd said it so sincerely at the time, that Amanda had believed her. (They had, after all, been playmates all through preschool, spending hours in the treehouse in

Lucy's backyard.) But now, with five long weeks between them, Amanda was pretty sure that Lucy had forgotten her completely.

Amanda's mom drove on in silence, and a few minutes later they passed George Washington Middle School. Some eager administrator had just changed the sign out in front from:

HAVE A EAT UMMER

to

WELCOME BACK TO SCHOOL

F1RST DAY — SEPT 4

"You know, Mom," said Amanda, sitting up and clearing her throat, "I was thinking . . . maybe we should try out homeschooling."

"Excuse me?" her mom said, glancing over at Amanda in disbelief. "Did you say *homeschooling*?"

"Uh . . ." Amanda bit her lip. "Yeah."

"Are you serious?" her mom continued. "*Me? Teach you?*" Then she let out one of the loud "Ha!"s that served as her form of laughter.

Amanda sat back. "Yeah, you're right. Maybe not."

Her mom slowed and turned into the driveway of the music school — an old, stately house that had once belonged to the mother of a U.S. president.

"Amanda?" said her mom, cutting the engine and turning in her seat. "What's all this about? Do you not want to go back to GW this fall?" Both her face and her voice were full of concern. It was an expression that Amanda knew meant her mother loved her — but it still had a way of driving her crazy every time she saw it.

"No, Mom," Amanda said. (Was that another lie?) "It's not that at all."

"Well, what is it, sweetie? Tell me?"

"*Mom,*" groaned Amanda. "It's *nothing*!" At least nothing she was prepared to share. "I mean, is it so weird to want to try something new every now and then?"

Her mom pursed her lips. Amanda could tell she was far from convinced — which left Amanda with only one option.

She unfastened her seat belt and reached for the door handle.

"I've gotta go, Mom!" she said. "I can't be late. Would Yo-Yo Ma's mother make him late by holding him hostage in the car?" She opened the door, grabbed her cello from the trunk, and swiftly slipped away.

Chapter Three

From: AllieOop@cablewest.com
To: Hays3@amerimail.com
Sent: Friday, August 31, 2007 8:54 AM
Subject: HERE I COME!

Hey there! Tomorrow is the big day! :-D I'm send-
ing this early, before I have to pack up the
computer, just to say that we should get there
sometime in the late afternoon. 505 Elm Street.
    See you there! I haven't seen the new digs
yet, but my mom says there's a tree house in the
backyard. Cool! Uh-oh! Gotta go. My dad's about to
pull the plug!
YBFF (and soon-to-be neighbor!),
Allie
OBTW — I am SO dying to meet John! ;-)

Amanda sighed. She was dying, too — of guilt!

Of course, she was excited. And she made sure to be down the street (at Lucy Milner's old house!) to meet Allie the very minute the moving van pulled up. She even begged her mom to let Allie sleep over that night, and her mom not only said yes, but suggested inviting Allie's whole family over for a cookout, too.

Everything went great — their parents got along well, and Allie's big brother was cool (he didn't tease her constantly, like Kate's always did). He even said again how good he thought Amanda was in the camp talent show. Allie's parents, and even Amanda's, agreed.

"Who knew when she came home from cello camp we'd have an improv comic on our hands?" her mom said, grinning.

"She gets it all from me!" put in her dad.

So everything was going perfectly. And Allie — no surprise — was just as fun and easy to be with as ever.

But things took a turn when Amanda showed Allie her room after dinner.

Right away, Allie went over to the mirror and pointed at the photo of the two of them laughing, arm in arm.

"Hey, you put up the picture I sent you!" she

said. "Oh, and there's the one of you and Kate. I am *so* dying to meet her!" She spun around, smiling brightly. "Can we call her? She could come over and spend the night, too!"

"Uh . . ." Amanda hesitated. She'd actually thought of that — for a second. But then she'd quickly ruled out the idea. On Allie's first night in town, she wanted her all to herself. That way, it would be a little bit like camp again . . . plus she figured this had to be the night that she confessed the truth about John.

"Actually, no, she can't," said Amanda. "Uh . . . my mom would probably think it's too much."

"You think?" Allie asked.

"Oh, yeah." Amanda nodded. "For sure. And besides, she's probably . . . um . . . out with her family. She has a lot of brothers and sisters and, uh, there's always a birthday or something to celebrate."

Now why did I say that? thought Amanda. *Why did I tell* more *lies?* Was she pathological or something? This had to stop — now.

"Ah, too bad," Allie said, turning back around. "Oh, I love this picture!" She pointed to one of Amanda and Kate smiling out from a pair of stockades.

"We took it in Williamsburg last year," said Amanda.

There. She *could* tell the truth. Phew.

"Cool!" said Allie. She paused before going on. "Hmm . . . but you know what I don't see here?"

"What?" said Amanda.

"I don't see a picture of John!"

Amanda gulped and took a deep breath. This was it. This was her moment of truth, at last.

Sure, she'd had weeks to break the news via e-mail. What could have been easier? And yet, she'd kept putting it off. Why? Had she thought that maybe sometime before Allie moved, Amanda would run into John somewhere — maybe he'd happen to ride his bike past her house — and they'd start talking and he'd actually end up being her boyfriend after all? Problem solved!

(Very) wishful thinking.

But that window of e-mail opportunity had come and gone, and she just couldn't keep up this dumb charade any longer.

"Actually, Allie —"

"Oh, here's one!" Allie picked up the photo of Amanda and John at Adventure Park from the dresser and held it up. "You must have more, though," she said, glancing around. "Where do you keep them? With all his letters, I bet! Hey, has he played you any new songs on his guitar? I swear," she said dreamily, "you are *so* lucky, Mandy. Do you even know how lucky you — wait a second!"

Suddenly, Allie's arm shot out and grabbed Amanda by the hand. "Let me see that!" she said, wide-eyed. "When did he give you *that*?"

Amanda looked down at the silver claddagh ring on her fourth finger, then back up into Allie's starry eyes. She looked so happy . . . so trusting . . . so easily disappointed. . . .

Amanda swallowed. "The other day," came out of her mouth before she could do anything to stop it.

"Wow," Allie sighed with a glowing smile. "But wait! You've got to turn it around."

She slipped the ring off Amanda's finger and turned it so the heart faced in.

"Much better," she went on. "You know, the other way means you're single."

"Oh, right," said Amanda, nodding. She closed her eyes. *Help!*

"So!" Allie bubbled, pulling a pack of gum out of her pocket and jumping back on Amanda's bed. "Spill! How did he give you the ring? Tell me the whole story — and don't leave out a thing!"

Luckily, just then, the phone rang and less than a minute later, Amanda's mom knocked on the door.

"Telephone," she said. "It's Kate. You know, we should have invited her, too. You can still ask her now, if you want." She smiled at the idea and handed over the receiver. "It's fine with me. Can I get you anything, Allie?"

"No thanks, Mrs. H. I ate *way* too many hot dogs. But it's a great idea to ask Kate over! Right, Mandy? Don't you think?"

Wincing, Amanda didn't respond. Instead, she took the phone from her mother and raised it slowly to her ear.

"Hey, Kate," she said. "Um . . . what are you up to?"

"Not much," came Kate's voice, just as awkwardly, from the other end of the line. "I was actually calling to see if you wanted to go to a movie. My brother's meeting a friend, and my mom's making him take some of us with him. But I guess . . . you have company?"

"Uh, yeah, kind of," said Amanda. "It's my friend, Allie, you know, from camp? I told you she was moving today . . . didn't I?" Amanda tried not to cringe, knowing that she hadn't told Kate this at all.

"No!" said Kate. There was a pause. "But I was wondering when she was coming. That's awesome. You know, she could totally come to the movies, too. Our van has plenty of room."

"Mmm . . . I don't know. . . ." Amanda mumbled, turning toward the wall. She lowered her voice to something *just* above a whisper. "She's awfully tired. Moving day and all."

"So does Kate want to come over?" Allie called from the across the room. "The night is young!"

Amanda shook her head and turned back around. "Uh-oh," she said to Kate. "I think I hear my mom calling. So . . . thanks for the invite, Kate. I'll totally tell Allie 'Hi' for you. Have a great time at the movie. Bye."

Amanda punched the phone's END button, then set it on her nightstand and guiltily backed away.

"She can't come?" asked Allie, looking disappointed.

Amanda shook her head and shrugged. "She's busy. Busy, busy, busy. But, uh . . . oh, she does say 'Hi,' and, um, she'll see you soon, I guess."

Allie sighed. "Oh, well. So, did you want to go find your mom?"

"Why?" Amanda asked. What did her mom have to do with anything?

"You said you heard her calling you? She's really cool, you know."

"Oh . . . right." Amanda nodded. Oh, brother. "Yeah. I did think I heard her call . . . Did you? But I don't hear her now, so maybe I was wrong."

"Good," said Allie, grinning. "Then we can get back to talking about John!"

Chapter Four

From: <u>AllieOop@amerimail.com</u>
To: <u>Hays3@amerimail.com</u>
Sent: Sunday, September 2, 2007 8:04 PM
Subject: GUESS WHAT?!

My mom just said she could take us to the
mall tomorrow to buy clothes for school. ;-)
Can you go? They should be having sales. Too
bad John's on an Eagle Scout campout this weekend.
I was hoping to meet him before school started.
But I guess that's just 2 days away,
anyway! :-)
YBFF,
Allie
OBTW — I am so nervous!!!

Amanda let out a short "Ha!" just like her mother's laugh. *Allie* was nervous? What about her? Two more days till school, and two more days till she was totally busted.

There must be something really wrong with her — how could she lie like that to Allie's face? It just made her friend so happy, it was impossible to tell her the truth. Well, not impossible . . . but really, really hard! Today was the day, though. It was Amanda's last chance before school started, and maybe the mall was the perfect place.

She could confess, casually, while they were shopping. And then they could laugh about it over a smoothie, or maybe a slice of pizza with extra cheese. They'd be having way too great of a time for Allie to get mad. And if she did, maybe Amanda could buy her an ice cream or something. . . .

She closed her e-mail and headed to the den, where her parents were watching TV.

"Hey, Mom?" she asked. "Would it be okay if I went to the mall with Allie and her mom tomorrow?"

Her mom looked up. "Sure," she said. "What are we doing tomorrow, Mark?" She turned to Amanda's dad. "Anything?"

"Hmm?" he mumbled, pretty much asleep in his armchair.

Her mom rolled her eyes. "Never mind. It's fine with me, Amanda." She lowered her voice. "But maybe don't mention it to your father. You know how he feels about that place and all those chain stores putting independent shops like his out of business. Oh, and make sure you leave plenty of time to practice your cello tomorrow, okay? Orchestra starts as soon as school does, right? And I know how important it is to you to make first chair."

Amanda nodded. "Don't worry. I'll make sure to practice."

It was funny, though. Until her mom mentioned it, Amanda hadn't thought about making first chair once since camp that summer. And before that, it had seemed so important! She still enjoyed her lessons, and she still had a good time playing. But there was so much else to think about. Did she *really* care about making first chair?

She turned to find the phone and call Allie, but her mother suddenly called her back into the den.

"Maybe," she said, "you should ask if Kate could go, too. She's such a sweetheart, and it would be a good way for Allie to make another friend before school starts. They seem like they'd get along so well." She cocked her head and offered Amanda an encouraging smile.

"Yeah . . . I guess," said Amanda slowly. She bit her lip and turned to walk away once more. Her mom was right, of course. That was just the thing a good friend would do. But it wasn't going to happen. She couldn't have Kate along when she finally confessed the truth to Allie!

Besides, Amanda wasn't so sure her mom was right about the two girls getting along. They were so totally different, they'd probably drive each other crazy. It was best not to force them together. Amanda was . . . pretty sure of that.

Late the next morning, Amanda introduced Allie to her town's only mall, which always reminded her of a terrarium — only bigger, and with stores. Allie's mom needed a ton of stuff for their new house, so she gave Allie a credit card (along with a firm, "Don't you dare buy anything I wouldn't!") and told the girls to meet her by the food court at two o'clock.

"So, where should we go?" Allie asked Amanda, slipping the credit card into her purse.

Amanda honestly wasn't sure. Her family did most of their shopping downtown, near her dad's store. Her dad, especially, thought the mall was "harmful to the town's soul." And maybe he was right. But it sure had a better selection of clothes!

"Um . . ." she began.

"Let's try this place!" said Allie, pointing.

She headed straight for a silver-framed store with a chorus line of well-dressed, headless dummies in the window, and Amanda happily followed.

"Bummer," observed Allie with a frown as they walked in. "All the fall clothes are out already, and it's still so *hot* . . . . Oh! But this is cute."

She held up a pale-blue tunic that automatically looked awesome with her cool blue eyes. "What do you think?"

"I *like* it," said Amanda. And she really did — a lot.

"Look, it's on sale," Allie noted. "My mom will like that!" Then she held out the top and looked at it critically. "You don't think it's too much for the first day of school, do you?" she asked. "I mean, you've gotta tell me, Mandy, what do people *wear* on the first day at GW?"

Good question, thought Amanda. It was something she also wondered about. Last year, she'd gone through at least a dozen outfits before settling on a matching skirt and top her aunt had sent her for her birthday. She'd barely gotten out the front door, though, when she turned around and ran back in. Way too dressy, she had decided. And so, with her dad hollering from the hallway, she'd changed into jeans and an old pink polo.

"You're wearing that?" her mom had said as she hugged and kissed her good-bye.

"Now don't go convincing her to change again," her dad had warned. "She's going to be late already."

It wasn't till she got to school that Amanda realized her wrinkled shirt had a faded trail of chocolate ice-cream stains running down the front. She was careful to keep a notebook in front of her chest for the rest of the day.

That was how *her* adventures in middle school fashion began. So who was she to give Allie advice now?

"Well, I think . . ." Amanda started.

"You're right!" Allie said. "Who cares? It's all about what you feel comfortable in, isn't it? And check this out!" She pulled a skirt off the rack that went perfectly with her top. "I am totally sold. With some sandals, and maybe a scarf?"

"I love it," said Amanda. "Go try it on."

"And what about you?" Allie pointed out. "We need something for you to try on, too."

Amanda looked around. There were lots of cute things she could try. . . . She picked up a shirt with LOVE written in gothic letters, and another with a row of ruffles along the bottom.

"You like?" she asked.

"Definitely," said Allie. "Oh! Hey, hey, *hey*! What about this?"

She glided over to another rack, picked out a shirt, and held it up for Amanda to see. It was silky black, with pink Chinese flowers running all over it. Little knotted buttons ran up the side. It reminded Amanda of a dress her parents had brought back from Hong Kong years ago. She'd loved it so much, she'd probably worn it to kindergarten every day for a month.

"I really like it, but . . . I don't know."

It was nice. But she knew it was different from what most kids at school wore.

It really was nice, though.

"Well, how would you know unless you tried it on?" said Allie. "Come on. With your hair — oh, it's going to look *so* awesome. You could wear it with a skirt and leggings. That would look cool! And you have black flats, don't you?"

Amanda nodded. Black flats for orchestra, of course.

"Well then, come on!" Allie grabbed Amanda's hand and pulled her toward the dressing rooms.

Amanda tried on the shirt, along with several other outfits. But it was the shirt, by far, that she loved the most.

"You *so* have to get it," Allie told her.

That was all it took.

And so, toting crisp, bulging bags and wearing the smiles of successful shoppers, the girls emerged from the store ready to take on the world.

"And now for accessories!" said Allie, pointing across the mall.

"Lead on!" Amanda called.

She wondered if maybe now was the time to bring up their absolutely, positively hilarious misunderstanding. But the second they stepped into the tiny accessory store, she knew the truth would have to wait. Accessorizing was simply too overwhelming.

What the store lacked in space, it more than made up for in inventory. The walls were lined from floor to ceiling with every kind of glittering barrette and headband and bracelet and earrings ever made.

Amanda quickly zeroed in on a pair of sparkly pink barrettes. How great would they look with her new outfit?

She checked the price. $9.99. She had just enough money left over to buy them, not counting the money she'd put aside for lunch. Clearly, the whole outfit was meant to be!

"What'd you find?" asked Allie, appearing at her side. "Oh, how cute! And look at these." She held up a stack of jangly bracelets, then slipped them on and let them clank back and forth along her wrist. "They'll hear *me* coming, won't they?"

"They're great," Amanda laughed. "Oh!" She pulled a bright blue plastic, jawbreaker-sized beaded necklace off the wall and draped it around her neck. "Who am I?" She sucked her cheeks in super tight and opened her eyes as wide as she could.

"Spindle Kindall!" Allie laughed, referring to *Doctor* Marla Kindall, one of the music counselors at camp. How her birdlike body supported all the heavy jewelry she always wore, they'd never understand!

"Too bad we didn't have that necklace for the talent show," Allie said. "Hey, check it out! They pierce ears here! Want to?"

Amanda followed Allie's gaze to the sign behind the counter.

EARS PIERCED

FREE WITH PURCHASE OF EARRINGS

It was tempting. She wondered how much a pair of earrings cost. But she also knew that if she came home with them in her ears, her mom would completely flip out.

"I don't know . . ." said Amanda. "I think my mom would kill me."

"Yeah." Allie nodded thoughtfully. "Mine probably would, too."

Laughing, Amanda set her hands primly on her hips. "'You may get your ears pierced when you turn thirteen,'" she mimicked her mom, "'and not a minute sooner!'"

"Exactly!" Allie giggled.

Another round of purchases made and two hours still ahead of them, the girls stepped into the heart of the mall and considered their options.

"I don't know about you," said Allie, "but I'm starving."

"Food court?" said Amanda. "Right this way."

As they rode down the escalator, it occurred to Amanda that *now* might be the perfect time to bring up the subject of John. But then she also realized that for the first time, Allie hadn't brought up the subject once.

What if, she thought optimistically, *Allie forgot about John? Yeah, right. Not likely.* But maybe, if they could just not talk about him anymore, Allie *would* forget about him. Maybe.

Together, they reached the bottom of the escalator, and without any discussion, made a beeline for the smoothie stall.

"Remember that smoothie machine at camp?" asked Allie.

"Oh, yeah!" said Amanda. "And remember how Ms. Matthews used to always, always spill them? 'Oh dear. Oh dear. We need a mop here. Oh dear!'"

Allie laughed and Amanda glanced up at the menu board.

Now, what should I get? she thought, deluged by the choices as always. *Mango Madness? Berry Breeze?* What she *really* felt like was watermelon. . . .

"Hey!"

All of sudden, Amanda felt a hard, sharp squeeze on her upper arm.

"*Ow!*" she cried. "What is it?"

"Look!" Allie said. "By the pretzels. Ten o'clock."

Curious, Amanda followed Allie's directions. "What?" she said, bewildered. There were pretzels. And people. And people with pretzels.

"*John!*" Allie said in a whisper so loud Amanda

was sure every shopper had heard it in every corner of the mall.

Amanda peered a little harder. *Oh my gosh,* she thought, her stomach instantly flipping over. *That is John. Oh no. No. NO!*

"Um . . . I don't think so," she said, turning back toward the counter. "So what kind of smoothie do *you* want?"

"Are you kidding?" Allie squealed. "It totally is! He's even wearing the same shirt he wore in your roller coaster picture." She looked at Amanda eagerly. "I guess his campout ended early. Lucky us! Come on, let's go say 'hi'!"

Amanda rubbed her forehead. Was she sweating? She felt like she was sweating. A lot.

"But don't you want to get a smoothie?" she asked, trying her best to sound calm. "I mean, look at the line. It'll take us forever to get to the front if we leave the line now."

Allie grinned. "You're sweet. But I can wait for a smoothie. I *can't* wait to meet John!"

Amanda turned to Allie and looked into her eager, trusting eyes.

I have to tell her, she thought. *I have to tell her right now.*

"Okay," she sighed weakly instead, stepping

slowly away from the smoothie line. "Let's go, I guess."

As they walked past the crowded food court tables, an image came to Amanda's mind. It was from a book about Marie Antoinette that she'd seen at the library over the summer. There was a picture at the end of the book showing Marie Antoinette riding to the guillotine — which was the exact feeling Amanda had at that very moment. *How did she even keep her head up?* Amanda wondered, as her own head hung miserably low.

"You lucky dog!" Allie leaned over and hooked her arm through Amanda's. "He's even cuter in person!"

Amanda looked up at the boy they were slowly but surely approaching. He was standing with three other guys she recognized from school. She knew the names of maybe two of them. *Matt and Cole?* she thought.

By now, they had gotten their pretzels and were dousing them in mustard and anything else free and sticky they could get their hands on. John was laughing at some joke, and the unnamed kid was fake gagging. If Amanda hadn't been concentrating so hard on her imminent doom, she would have assumed that they were making fun of her. There was always a bright side.

All too soon, there was just one trash can left between them. Amanda racked her brain; she had no clue what to say or do. She took one more step forward — then watched in amazement as the boys turned and, stuffing their faces, ambled off the other way.

"Huh?" said Allie, throwing her hands up in disbelief. She spun to look at Amanda with wide eyes. "What's up with that? Did he not see you or something?"

"I guess not!" said Amanda, trying not to sound *too* relieved.

But Allie wasn't giving up quite so easily.

"Yoo-hoo!" she shouted after the boys, waving her arms.

The boy on John's left turned to look, staring blankly past the two girls. Then he spun back around and kept walking.

"Well, that was *weird.*" Allie frowned. "I mean, really . . ."

Amanda shrugged, but didn't answer. She could have come clean so easily right then, and she knew it. But instead, she suddenly had a totally new and different plan. . . .

Chapter Five

From: <u>AllieOop@amerimail.com</u>
To: <u>Hays3@amerimail.com</u>
Sent: Monday, September 3, 2007 6:43 PM
Subject: Re: sad news

No way! I can't believe you and John broke up! :0
What happened? Call me when you get back from your
grandparents and tell me everything ASAP! I am SO
sorry! :'(
YBFF,
Allie

    Amanda sighed. So, it was done. She and John
had officially broken up.

    Why hadn't she thought of it before? Why

confess a lie when making up a new one could solve the problem?

She'd actually gotten the idea at the mall, but had waited until later that afternoon to send an e-mail to Allie, breaking the tragic news. (E-mail was so much easier than having to tell another lie in person!)

Now, after dinner at her grandparents' house, Amanda figured it was only fair to call Allie.

Allie picked up the phone on the very first ring.

"Mandy!" she said, concern filling her normally carefree voice. "What happened? I *so* knew there was something going on today at the mall!"

Amanda let out a breath that she hoped sounded appropriately heavy. "Yeah," she said.

"And to think I thought you guys were so perfect for each other!" Allie sighed. "Do you think you'll stay friends?"

Amanda wasn't sure what to say. "Uh . . ."

"If you don't want to talk about it, I understand," Allie went on.

Amanda cleared her throat. This was her out! "Yeah, I'd rather not. But I'm fine. After all, you know what they say: There are a lot more fish in the sea!"

51

"You are *so* right," said Allie. "And we'll go fishing in the morning!"

After chatting a bit more (but not about John — *whew!*), Amanda hung up, relieved. But it wasn't long before she began to wonder if telling yet another lie to cover up her first one truly *was* the smartest move. (It sure hadn't kept that old guilty feeling from crawling back.) Still, it did make going to school the next day a little easier.

And the first morning of seventh grade, in fact, started off very well.

Allie and Amanda discovered that they were in the same homeroom, with everyone's favorite history teacher, Mr. Morrison. They hadn't even chosen their seats when a tall, friendly girl walked up.

"I'm Henley," she said to Allie. "You're new this year, aren't you? I wanted to say hi — I *really* love your skirt."

Amanda noticed that the girl was wearing a pretty nice skirt herself. She had long, layered brown hair and a tan. It was none other than Henley Mossbach, one of Lucy Milner's old friends and another one of the prettiest, most popular girls in school.

"Thanks!" Allie said, gesturing to Amanda.

"Mandy helped me pick it out! I didn't know what to wear to a new school and all. I was *so* nervous. My name's Allie."

"Hi," Henley smiled at Allie through her straight, white teeth, then turned her gaze on Amanda. "Hi. How was your summer, Mandy? You know, I'd always thought it was Amanda. Hey! I love your top, too."

Amanda couldn't help but blush. Henley Mossbach liked her shirt!

"Want to sit with us over there?"

Amanda looked to where Henley was pointing: a cluster of desks filled with other girls just as carefree-looking and perfectly dressed as her. It was exactly the kind of scene Amanda (and Kate) would normally have shied away from. After all, those girls couldn't be interested in someone like her. They had all the friends they needed.

"Yeah, totally!" said Allie. She followed after Henley, dragging Amanda by the hand.

"Hey, guys," said Henley. "I want you to meet Allie. And you remember Mandy? Don't you just *love* her top?"

"Hey!" one of the girls said.

"Ooh! That's so pretty!"

"Where did you get it?"

And suddenly, before Amanda knew it, there they were — all of them — talking and laughing about shopping and the summer and being back at school. Everyone wanted to know all about Allie. She was more than happy to share her story, including the part about meeting "Mandy" at camp, and what great friends they had become.

"There is absolutely, positively no better roommate in the world!" said Allie. "Remember that time the boys broke into our room?" she asked Amanda. "And kidnapped Bear-Bear? You totally got him back."

"Oh yeah!" Amanda laughed. She nodded to the girls. "The guys must have snuck in while we were at dinner or something. They left a ransom note."

"A ransom note!" said Henley. "What did it say?"

"I quote," Amanda said, lowering her voice an octave. " 'Dear Allie, We have your bear. If you ever want to see it again in one 'peace' (misspelled!), leave a box of Pop Tarts outside the tennis courts tonight. P.S. Do not tell the authorities.' "

"No way!" Henley's friend Megan cried.

"Way!" Allie responded, grinning. "So tell them what you did, Amanda."

"Well," said Amanda. "I was pretty sure I knew who took Bear-Bear." She grinned at the girls and Allie, who was blushing and shaking her head.

"There was this one guy," Amanda went on, "who had a massive crush on her . . ."

Allie made a face. "*Not* reciprocated!" she spat.

Amanda giggled. "No, not at all. Anyway, I figured he was a pretty reliable suspect, so the next day, when we were all supposed to be in workshops, I took an extra long bathroom break and ran back to the boys' dorm. Sure enough, I found the bear in his room."

"Poor Bear-Bear," said Allie, pouting.

"Classic!" said Henley. "Tell us more!"

And Allie happily obliged.

Amanda, meanwhile, sat back for a moment and pinched herself. Was she dreaming? The day had hardly begun and already her outfit had been a huge success, and she was sitting with a whole group of the most popular girls. It was too good to be true — almost.

That's when *he* walked into the room. John.

"Hey, loser!" yelled his friend Cole, waving to him across the room.

"Who are you calling a loser?" John called back, laughing and jogging over to give Cole a high five. He could not have passed any closer to Amanda, and he could not have ignored her more.

"Wow," Allie leaned over and whispered. "You guys really aren't talking, are you?"

Amanda bit her lip and self-consciously shook her head.

"They probably don't even know yet," whispered Allie, nodding to the other girls.

Amanda quickly shook her head and put a finger to her lips. Suddenly, she wished she really *was* dreaming.

Then, thankfully, the bell rang to mark the start of homeroom.

"Good mornin'!" said Mr. Morrison, in a cheerful voice. He had big hair and an even bigger mustache. *If walruses wore wigs and were born in the South,* Amanda thought, *he could definitely pass for one.*

"Now, I'm goin' to pass out some name tags to y'all, and I want you to fill 'em out. I know y'all know one another just fine. But trust me, the faster I can learn your names, the happier I'll be." He gazed around with a great big grin on his face. "And y'all want me to be happy."

They all filled out name tags and slapped them haphazardly on their shirts. And *that* was how Amanda discovered she'd been misspelling her "boyfriend's" name for half the summer. *Oh, no, no, no!* she thought, looking over at "Jon"'s name tag in horror.

"Check it out," Allie whispered when she noticed the missing "h." She shrugged at Amanda as if to say, "What gives?"

Amanda rolled her eyes and shrugged back. (It was the only thing that she could think to do!)

Then she looked down at her own name tag and wondered how many people were probably commenting on *that* one. She'd very nearly written "Amanda," out of a lifetime of habit. But then she'd stopped . . . and slowly written M-A-N-D-Y. After all, practically half the class had started to call her that already.

She wondered if she'd have felt different if Kate were there to see her. She'd already gotten the eyebrow raise when Kate read her new nickname in Allie's e-mail. Who was she kidding, anyway? She was Amanda — smart, quiet, under-the-radar Amanda. The only thing Kate would think, if she saw her now, was that "Mandy" was some kind of wannabe phony.

But she doesn't understand, thought Amanda. *This is me. I mean . . . I think it is.*

Or maybe Kate would be jealous. Amanda knew that if she were Kate, she probably would have been. . . .

She smoothed the corners of her name tag,

where it seemed most opposed to sticking to her silky shirt, and sat back to listen to Mr. Morrison call roll.

Amanda had to admit, she was relieved that she didn't have to worry about her stupid Jo(h)n lie *and* Kate, too.

At least, not yet.

Chapter Six

DEAR MANDY,

Hi THERE. WRITING TO YOU FROM GYM, WAITING FOR GYM SUITS TO BE HANDED OUT. TOO BAD WE DON'T HAVE THIS CLASS TOGETHER. BOO-HOOOO! BUT GUESS WHO I <u>DO</u> HAVE IT WITH? JOHN! (I DON'T CARE IF HE CHANGED THE SPELLING. I'M KEEPING THAT H ALIVE!) AND YOU KNOW WHAT? I CAN TOTALLY SEE WHY YOU BROKE UP WITH HIM. HE IS SOOOO IMMATURE! I THINK RIGHT NOW HE'S BALANCING A CONE ON HIS HEAD. AND THEN HE GOES AND ACTS LIKE HE HARDLY EVEN KNOWS YOU IN HOMEROOM AND THE HALLS! I SOOOO WANTED TO TELL HIM OFF!

THERE! I JUST GAVE HIM THE EVIL EYE FOR YOU. UH-OH! HERE COME THE GYM SUITS. GOTTA GO!
XXXOOO
ALLIE

Amanda folded the note back up and slipped it into her purse as she hurried down the hall.

Ugh. So Allie and Jon (Seriously, who knew he didn't spell it with an "h"?) shared a class without her. Well, at least it was gym, where the boys and girls were separated most of the time.

With her throat tightening, she wondered if they'd share the next class, too. What did Allie have? Math? And then, of course, there was lunch with *all* the seventh graders. What *that* would bring, Amanda could only dread.

It could bring Kate and Allie together, for one thing — a meeting Amanda had been avoiding, though neither one of them knew why.

She knew it would be tricky the minute she walked into the cafeteria with Kate and picked up her plastic tray.

"Hey, there you are! How was gym? Oh, hey! You must be Kate!"

Amanda and Kate turned to see Allie hurrying up to the line.

"Oh, I'm glad you're just getting here, too," she said, halfway panting. "I went to find my locker and totally got lost!" She laughed and turned

60

to Kate. "Hey, Kate! I'd know you anywhere! I'm Allie!"

Allie offered her hand, and Kate happily shook it. "Hi," she replied. "Welcome to GW. It's nice to meet you."

"Thanks." Allie grinned. "It is *so* great to meet you! So, what's the food like?" She grabbed a tray and scanned the food with hungry eyes. "As long as they have pizza, I'm totally good."

"Oh, they have pizza," said Amanda. "But don't say anything until you've tried it." She made a face as she reached for a bag of fries. "Uh . . . how was math, Allie? Pretty good?"

"Yeah," replied Allie. "It was okay. No *Jon* in that class, at least." She grinned sympathetically.

Amanda quickly cut her eyes to assess Kate's reaction. Thankfully, Kate had moved ahead to the salad bar.

The three girls filled their trays and marched out into the din of the middle school lunchroom. *Whoa!* Amanda had forgotten how loud it was!

Kate walked straight toward the little table in the corner where she and Amanda had sat all last year. For some reason — maybe because it was so far from the lunch line, or so close to the trash — it had always been available. It looked like this year wouldn't be any different.

Amanda followed Kate instinctively, then stopped as Allie called her back.

"Hey, Mandy! Hang on!" Allie hollered. "There's Henley and Jen. We can sit with them."

Amanda turned to see Henley and a bunch of her friends waving from an enviably loud and cheerful table in the center of the room. It was a sight, she realized, she'd never seen before.

"Uh . . ." she began. She glanced back at the corner table, where Kate had already sat down.

"What?" Allie asked, confused.

"Well, Kate's sitting down over there. . . ."

"So call her back," Allie said. "Or I'll go get her."

"Oh, I don't know," Amanda said quickly. "There's probably not enough room at Henley's table. You stay, and I'll go sit with her," she said.

"Are you sure?" Allie asked, looking puzzled.

"Yeah, totally," said Amanda. "I'll see you after."

She turned with relief, and headed back in Kate's direction. But a moment later, she felt Allie back at her side.

Amanda looked at her, confused.

"What?" said Allie. "Of course I'm going to sit with you!"

Amanda sighed, though she couldn't help but smile.

"So!" Allie said to Kate, as she plopped down at the small table. "It's so great to finally meet you! Amanda told me so much about you this summer. I feel like you're my best friend, too!"

Amanda watched them share a smile, and couldn't help thinking, *Hey, this isn't so bad. . . .*

Then Allie winked. "Kept your bathing suit on for the rest of the summer, I hope."

Amanda cringed as Kate turned to shoot her with an *I'm-gonna-kill-you!* glare.

"So how was your morning, Kate?" Allie went on, blissfully unaware.

"Pretty good," Kate said slowly. She turned away from Amanda's apologetic face and took a sip of chocolate milk. "I have homeroom with Mrs. Brodsky, and she's okay. And history's good. . . . How 'bout you?"

"Oh, it's been great!" said Allie. She put her arm around Amanda. "I've got history with Mandy here. Hey! Don't you love her top?"

"Oh, yeah," Kate said, nodding. "I told her so already. It reminds me of this dress she used to wear all the time in elementary school."

Allie smiled a big, open smile. "We got it at the mall just yesterday," she said. "It was on sale. If you like it, they might have more."

Amanda closed her eyes, more than happy

that she hadn't erased her *I'm-so-sorry-Kate* face quite yet.

"Oh, but anyway," Allie went on, "I have Mitchell for math. She's kind of funny. And, oh!" She leaned forward, toward Kate. "Guess who I had gym with? John! And guess what? Have you heard this yet? This year he's decided to spell his name J-O-N. No 'h'!"

She grinned mischievously at Kate, who was clearly not sure what she was supposed to say.

Allie shook her head. "I know. It's weird."

"So," said Amanda, gulping to keep down her milk and desperate to change the subject. "What's on the rest of everybody's schedule? Do we have any more classes together?"

All three girls took out their schedules to compare.

"Oh, good, we have orchestra together," Kate said to Amanda. "And look, we all have English together. That's pretty cool."

"And what do you have before that?" asked Allie. "Spanish? With Barry?"

"Yeah," said Kate.

"Me, too. Cool!" Allie's smile grew even wider

"Is that 'LAT' what I think it is?" Kate asked, peering over at Amanda's schedule.

"Yep," said Amanda, nodding. "My mom made

64

me sign up for Latin. She said it would be helpful in learning all the other languages." She rolled her eyes, then wagged her finger, exactly like her mother. "'*Trust* me, Amanda. One day, you'll *thank* me.'"

Kate and Allie both laughed. Then Kate reached out and took Amanda by the hand.

"Hey, silly!" she said. "You're wearing your ring the wrong way again."

Amanda looked down and realized that she was still wearing her claddagh ring the way Allie had turned it: heart in, heart taken.

Kate smoothly slipped the ring off and put it back on the other way.

"There," she said as Amanda's heart tried to remember how to beat normally.

"I told her," Kate went on, smiling at Allie, "that if she wears the ring the other way, no one will know she's available!"

Amanda's eyes flashed to Allie. *Oh, no,* she thought. What would she say?

"Totally!" replied Allie. She nodded knowingly at Kate, then turned, to Amanda, concerned. "Are you sure you even want to wear it?" she asked.

If Kate's jaw hadn't been attached, it would have fallen to the floor.

"Ha!" Amanda choked. "Very funny. Wow, look at the time! We'd better shut up and eat!"

But, of course, Amanda couldn't keep them from talking — especially Allie. And no matter how hard she tried to redirect the conversation, before lunch was done, Kate knew all about the things Amanda and Allie had done without her.

"I so wish you could have gone shopping with us yesterday," Allie told her.

Kate frowned and glanced cooly at Amanda. "Yeah . . . me, too."

"And sometime we *all* have to have a sleepover, don't you think?" Allie continued, while Amanda wished she could crawl under the table and disappear.

At least Allie hadn't had time to get back to the subject of Jo(h)n. But who knew what might come out when Kate and Allie were alone? So Amanda took Allie aside right after lunch and told her how mean she'd heard Señora Barry was. But she said she'd heard that if you sat in the back row of Spanish class, Señora picked on you a lot less.

In fact, everyone did say Señora Barry was mean. (That was *not* a lie.) But Amanda didn't really think that any seat would make a difference. She just knew that Kate liked to sit in the front, and that it couldn't hurt to try to keep her and Allie apart.

Thankfully, science and English turned out

okay. But just as Amanda had feared, Jo(h)n was in not just one of those classes, but both!

The award for hardest class of the day, though, might have gone to orchestra. There, it was immediately apparent that Amanda had not been practicing nearly enough that summer. . . .

"Amanda, my goodneth," said Mrs. Havenov-Butz, the orchestra teacher (whose new married name was almost as amusing as her lisp). "I thought you would have had thith pieth down by the end of the thummer."

"Sorry, Mrs. Havenov," Amanda muttered.

"Havenov-*Butzth,*" the teacher reminded her. "Really, I would have exthpected more after three weekth of thello camp."

"Yeah . . . I know . . . you see . . ." Amanda tapped her bow against the side of her head. *Oh gosh,* she thought. She'd been worried about all kinds of things, but never once had she considered that the orchestra teacher might call her out like this. Of course, it made perfect sense. After all, Mrs. Havenov-Butz had helped her and Kate with their camp applications. While she'd heard about Kate having to pull out, she clearly thought that Amanda had been playing nonstop all summer.

"Yeth?" said the teacher.

"Oh, Mrs. Havenov-Butz," Kate called suddenly

from her seat in the flute section. "Didn't you say you were going to play us the CD you made in Italy this summer? I just wondered, 'cause the period's almost over."

"Ah, yeth." The teacher smiled. "I did want you to hear how we played in Thithily this thummer. Thank you, Kate. Here . . ."

While the teacher found her CD and dropped it into the player, Amanda turned to give Kate a grateful smile.

She owed her one . . . to say the least.

Whoever would have guessed that by the end of the day, Latin — the brand-new class her school was trying; the class which her mom had *made* her take; and the class which everyone, even Kate, had thought would be *way* boring — would end up being Amanda's favorite? The reason? Simple. No friends. No cello. And no secret boyfriend.

Chapter Seven

DEAR MANDY,

DON'T LOOK NOW, BUT DID YOU SEE THE WAY JOHN WAS STARING AT YOU A LITTLE WHILE AGO?! I TOTALLY CAUGHT HIM, AND HE TOTALLY BLUSHED! I THINK MAYBE HE WANTS YOU BACK! THAT'S GOT TO BE WHY HE'S ACTING SO WEIRD.

IN FACT, HERE'S WHAT I THINK: HE'S GOING TO ASK YOU TO THE BACK-TO-SCHOOL DANCE! WOULD YOU EVER GO? HEY, HOW DID I NOT NOTICE ANY OF THE SIGNS FOR THE DANCE YESTERDAY? AND WHEN WERE YOU GOING TO MENTION IT? REMEMBER HOW MUCH FUN THE DANCE AT CAMP WAS? (HEY, MACARENA!) I LOVE THIS SCHOOL!

YBFF,

ALLIE

OBTW—WHAT ARE DANCES HERE LIKE? AND WHAT ARE WE GOING TO WEAR?!

Amanda slipped the note into her history note-book and tried to look as interested in Mr. Morrison's thirteen colonies lesson as she could. Inside, though, she was laughing. What was the back-to-school dance like? How would she know? She'd never been.

Last year, she and Kate hadn't even thought about going. A dance? During the first week of middle school? With hundreds of people they didn't know? No thanks.

Amanda was pretty sure they'd watched a DVD that night instead, probably with Kate's little brother and sister. And though she'd noticed the signs for the dance on the first day of school this year, she hadn't given them much thought. But now, as Mr. Morrison walked around distrib-uting his handouts, she couldn't *stop* thinking about them.

Now that she was in seventh grade, the dance *could* be a lot of fun — especially with Allie.

Amanda hadn't exactly been looking forward to the dance at the end of camp, either. She didn't know how to dance, for one thing. It seemed like an awful lot of pressure — figuring out the right moves in front of *all* those people. But as Allie always did, she made it seem okay.

"You've got to dance!" Amanda remembered

Allie telling her. "You can't just stand here all night long!"

"You're right," said Amanda, as she glanced around the dining hall. "I think I'll go sit over there."

"Listen!" said Allie as a new song blared over the speakers. "It's the Macarena!" She grabbed Amanda's hand. "You have to know this one. . . . No? Well, I'm going to teach you!"

Then, before Amanda could do anything about it, Allie dragged her out onto the dance floor.

Twenty-five songs (and one ridiculous macarena) later, Amanda's shirt was completely drenched in sweat, her hair was a disaster area, she'd totally lost her shoes . . . and she'd had the most fun of her entire life.

It was funny, really. She'd been *making* music for as long as she could remember. But she'd never just let loose and enjoyed it so much!

Of course, camp was very different from school. There were way fewer people, and way less pressure to be so cool. At camp, everyone was her friend. At school, it seemed like everyone was somebody else's friend.

But that wasn't entirely true. She had Kate and her other old friends. And this year, she had Allie.

Amanda glanced over at Henley and Megan and Jen, who were sure to be going to the back-to-school dance, too.

Why not? she finally thought. Maybe she *would* go.

That said, the stuff in Allie's note about Jo(h)n liking her — *really* liking her — made her laugh. There was just no way! (Was there?)

Yes, she *had* seen Jo(h)n looking at her a few times, and at Allie, too. And yes, he had been acting pretty weird. That morning, he'd walked into the classroom with his backpack over his head yelling, "Who turned out the lights?" (That was just plain odd.) But then later, before the bell rang, he'd walked right up to them and very nearly started to speak. (*Eek!*) Allie had crossed her arms as if she dared him to say a word, and he'd turned and fled in silence.

What if he knows about my lie? Amanda wondered, panicking. She held her hand next to her face and slowly peered at him from around it. He was flicking bits of balled-up paper at his friend, Cole, who sat in front of him.

"Hey, Jon!" called Mr. Morrison. "When we get to the Battle of Lexington, I'd love to have ya act it out for us. Till then, though, cut it out. Or better yet, tell me somethin' about the Declaration of Independence."

Nah, Amanda decided. She was being silly. He was just a regular, goofy boy, who was to be *watched,* but not to be feared. And the dance wasn't something to be afraid of, either. With Allie, it was sure to be fun.

"You know, I was thinking," said Kate, pulling her itchy poly-blend gym shirt down over her head. "Maybe you could come over Friday so we could practice that piece that Mrs. You-Know-Who wants you to work on. Or we could even start working on something for the fall talent show." She neatly tucked the shirt into her shorts, then frowned and pulled it out. "I asked my mom last night, and she said it would be okay."

Amanda yanked on her own gym shirt, which was much too big — *again.*

"Friday?" she said. "You mean right after school?"

Kate shook her head. "No, I have to go to the orthodontist right after school. I was thinking after that. You could come for dinner, too."

"Oh . . . I don't know . . ." said Amanda. Friday. The night of the dance.

She sat down on the rickety locker room bench and started to tie her shoes. "I might have to do something else," she said, trying to sound casual. "How about . . . er . . . Saturday?"

"Mmm, probably not," Kate said. She gave her curls a yank to tighten her ponytail. "Saturday's Molly's eighth birthday. She's having a *bowling* party — remember those?" She laughed. "But you could come, too. She'd love that!"

Kate sat down next to Amanda and began to tie up her own shoes. "What do you have to do Friday?" she asked carefully.

"Uh . . ." Amanda looked down and busily double-knotted her laces.

What should she tell Kate she was doing? Dinner with her parents? What would seem most believable? *Wait a second!* Amanda thought. What was she doing? She already felt bad enough about the lies she'd told to Allie and all the secrets she'd kept from Kate. She couldn't tell her best friend another lie — and she definitely didn't want to!

Then again, it wasn't like Kate even wanted to go to the back-to-school dance. If it wasn't music or softball in the spring, it wasn't on Kate's radar. Kate might think Amanda was downright crazy for wanting to go. Or — and this was a thought she wasn't proud of — what if Kate wanted to tag along? Then what? Would Amanda have to stand around and talk to Kate, instead of dancing with Allie and Henley and her friends?

Amanda took a deep breath, stood up, and swung the door to her gym locker closed. She'd made up her mind.

"Oh, I'm just doing stupid stuff on Friday," she said with a shrug. "But how 'bout Sunday, instead? You can come over to my house. My dad'll cook out, I bet, and we'll have plenty of time to start thinking about the fall talent show. Any ideas?" she asked.

"Hmm . . ." Kate's forehead wrinkled the way it always did when she was concentrating on something. "You know, I actually learned a few Irish folk songs this summer. . . . They're pretty fun . . . but I don't know. Oh, wait! I do!" She grinned and the wrinkles melted away. "What about something *modern*? My sister played the coolest, prettiest song for me the other day. It's up on her MySpace page."

Amanda smiled at the suggestion, relieved that Kate didn't ask any more questions about Friday night. "That sounds good!" she said. "I'll listen to it tonight. Does she still have that goofy picture of herself up there, too?"

They laughed just as a whistle sounded from outside the locker room door.

"Coach Kelly calls," groaned Amanda.

"She's not that bad," giggled Kate.

"That's easy for you to say," said Amanda. "You're actually competent at gym. I can barely do a push-up."

"Oh, give me a break," laughed Kate. "Now get out there and give me twenty!"

Chapter Eight

DEAR MANDY,

JUST SITTING HERE IN ART THINKING ABOUT THE DANCE TONIGHT. I CANNOT <u>wait</u>! WHAT ARE YOU GOING TO WEAR? I'M THINKING MY NEW JEANS WOULD BE GOOD, BUT WHAT KIND OF TOP? YOU HAVE TO COME OVER AND HELP ME FIGURE IT OUT! MY MOM'S TAKING MY BROTHER TO A FOOTBALL GAME TONIGHT, BUT SHE SAID SHE COULD DROP US AT THE DANCE ON THE WAY. DO YOU THINK YOUR MOM COULD PICK US UP? OOPS! HAVE TO FINISH MY STILL LIFE BEFORE THE BELL RINGS!

YBFF

ALLIE,

OBTW — DO YOU THINK JOHN'S GOING TO GO? (I STILL WOULDN'T BE SURPRISED IF HE ASKS YOU!)

Well, I'd *be surprised!* thought Amanda. *I sure* hope *he's not going to go!*

She hadn't even considered *that* possibility before. Jon certainly didn't seem like a big dancer, though, so she tried not to worry about him too much as the day dragged on.

By the time they got to the dance (looking awesome, she had to say), Amanda was totally excited. It was a wonderful feeling that stayed with her for all of three and half minutes — until the horrible "multiplication dance" began.

"Welcome, students!" the principal, Mr. Hamm, hollered. He was standing under the basketball hoop, microphone in hand.

The hoop was one of the few things in the gym that Amanda recognized. Otherwise, it had been transformed (rather hastily) into a very dark, rather sweaty-smelling dance hall. All the shades were drawn and all the lights were off (except for two spotlights shining on a twirling mirror ball), making it hard to see more than a few dots-worth of the portly principal at any given time.

"Okay, then! I hope you all had a wonderful summer!" Mr. Hamm went on, pausing for a moment to slide his glasses back up the slippery slope of his thick nose. "I think I've gotten a chance to say 'Hi' to most of you this week. But if I haven't, I'll be here all night."

Amanda grinned at Allie. "Oh, boy!" she mouthed.

"Now, as you all know, the back-to-school dance is a proud tradition of George Washington Middle School, and we always like to kick it off with another proud tradition, the multiplication dance!"

A muffled chorus of moans and groans rumbled around the gym.

"What's a 'multiplication dance'?" asked Allie, leaning over to offer Amanda a piece of gum.

Amanda took it and shrugged. "No idea," she whispered back. "Maybe it's a dance-slash-pop-quiz or something?"

"Now, now," Mr. Hamm shushed the crowd. "Let's act like middle-schoolers. And for those who aren't familiar with this great icebreaker, let me explain." He cleared his throat and pushed his glasses up again. "It's simple, really. When the music starts, one couple will get out there on the dance floor and get things started." He did a little twist and grinned. "Then, when the DJ stops the music, that couple splits up. Each person goes and quickly chooses another partner before the music starts again. They'll dance together, then the DJ will stop the music again and those two couples will split up and each go find another partner. And on and on."

"I think we get the idea," whispered Amanda, frowning.

"Does everyone get the idea?" asked the principal. "Just remember. The whole point is to be a good sport. If someone asks you to dance, you may not say 'no.' Okay, then! DJ, some music, if you please!"

Amanda turned to Allie.

"Okay, then," she said. "I think it's time to go to the bathroom."

"Are you kidding?" said Allie. "*Now?* Don't you want to see who asks who to dance? Hey, look — Henley's starting it off! Who's she with? Is that an *eighth* grader?"

Amanda nodded. "Yeah, I think so." She watched the tall, blond boy lead Henley out onto the dance floor. A song filled the air, and Amanda immediately noted that it was *horrifyingly* slow. The boy held Henley's waist and she put her hands on his shoulders, and they swayed smoothly back and forth like they'd done it a million times before.

"Is he her boyfriend?" Allie asked.

"Looks like it," said Amanda. She sighed. How lucky could you get?

After a minute, the song stopped, and the boy and Henley turned around.

Conveniently, the crowd had already divided itself into two distinct parts: the boys' side and the girls' side. Amanda watched as the blond boy sauntered over toward the crowd of girls and offered his hand to a very pretty, dark-haired fellow eighth grader. Henley, meanwhile, had gone over to the boys' side and picked a cute guy, Will, who'd been class Vice President last year.

Amanda had to admit that if you didn't have to worry about being picked and having to slow-dance, it was pretty entertaining. Some of the couples made it look easy. Others made it look downright painful — particularly by the fifth round, when it was clear that most of the boys had no desire to be anywhere near a girl, and the girls had run out of boys who were taller than them.

That's also about when Amanda noticed a new figure out on the floor.

Jon.

"You know what?" she said, unable to hide the sudden urgency in her voice. "I really *do* have to go to the bathroom. See you in a sec."

But Allie grabbed her by the arm.

"Mandy!" she said. "Don't you dare! We went before we came in here. And look who's dancing — don't you want to see who he picks next?"

No, thought Amanda. *Not really.* But she stood there, anyway, and let out a heavy sigh. If only Allie's mom had dropped them off *after* taking her brother to the football game. Then they might have missed this miserable part!

"He's a pretty good dancer," said Allie with an approving nod.

Amanda watched Jon bobbing comfortably on the floor. No, he wasn't bad, it was true. Though he wasn't quite as good as Henley's boyfriend. . . . She let her eyes wander around the dance floor, searching for his blond head above the rest, and wondered with a nervous twinge what the chances were that he might ask *her* to dance before the end.

Then the music stopped again and Amanda felt Allie stiffly nudge her in the ribs.

"What did I tell you?" Allie hissed. "He's coming!"

Amanda looked up. *Who? Oh, no!*

Not Henley's cute boyfriend, but — *allegedly* — her own!

She swallowed hard and rubbed her hands on the ruffled skirt she'd borrowed from Allie. Her hands weren't sweaty, were they? It wasn't like she really, truly liked Jon. But if he really did like *her*, well, she didn't want to freak him out.

Did he really like her? Could anything so weird be true?

And did she maybe in some weird, subconscious way, like him, too? Is that why she let Allie think he was her boyfriend? Maybe she was more than just a big, fat liar. Maybe she and Jon were, in fact, really meant to be together?

Then, all of a sudden, another thought raced through her head: *How do you dance, again?*

But before she could recall a single move, Jon was standing in front of them, reaching out his hand, and opening up his mouth to speak . . .

To Allie.

"Hey. Do you . . . uh . . . want to dance?"

Allie stared at Jon, then turned to Amanda in confusion. "Who? *Me?*" she said.

Jon nodded. "Uh, *yeah.* The music's starting."

Allie looked at Amanda again, and Amanda stared back just as bewildered.

Then — what could she do? — Amanda shrugged and said, "Go, dance."

In a daze, Allie followed Jon out to the dance floor, and Amanda stood and watched them go. She crossed her arms in front of her chest and tried to process what had just happened. Well, at least she didn't have to wonder if she and Jon were soulmates anymore. But as she watched them dancing, Allie glaring at Jon, she realized she had something even more serious to worry about. What if Allie said something to him?!

Please, please, she silently pleaded, *please don't say anything to Jon! Please don't say anything like "You really need to get over Mandy," or "She's never going to get back together with you if you keep treating her this way." Please!*

Fortunately, aside from blowing one big, hostile bubble in Jon's unsuspecting face, Allie's mouth stayed in a tight, straight line throughout their section of the dance. Then, as Amanda watched, she fixed Jon with one more icy scowl and turned with a flip of her curls to pick a partner of her own.

Amanda sighed. *That* was close. She'd hoped that "breaking up" with Jon would make the whole stupid lie go away. But she had been sorely mistaken. And now, instead of one lie to cover up, she had more. That wasn't even counting the lies she'd told Kate.

Poor Kate, thought Amanda, her regrets multiplying even faster than the miserable dance. Of course she'd find out that Amanda had gone to the dance. She was probably calling her house right now, to find that Amanda wasn't there.

"Well, hi, Kate," her mom was probably saying. "No, I'm sorry. Amanda's not home. She's at the back-to-school dance with Allie. Weren't you going, too?"

Then Kate would probably start debating whether she should burn all the mementos she'd ever collected of their friendship, or simply toss them in the trash.

Yes, Kate had taken the news about Amanda's sleepover and shopping trip with Allie pretty well. But those hadn't been outright lies, either. Amanda had just tried to keep them a secret. But this . . .

What was she turning into? What had she already become? And what was she doing, standing there by the bleachers, waiting to be the last girl picked to dance?

It was definitely the right time to go to the bathroom. But just as she turned around, she felt a hand fall on her shoulder.

"Amanda?"

She turned her head to see the wide, dimpled smile of Evan Skelpe — the one boy she knew from orchestra who was also taking Latin. (Apparently their mothers came from the same make-the-kids-suffer-as-much-as-possible School of Parenting.)

"Dance?" he asked.

"Uh . . ." Amanda made a face that she knew came across as less than thrilled. But then she reeled it in, forced a smile, and nodded.

"Sure," she said.

"I don't want to *torture* you or anything," said Evan.

Amanda laughed. "Sorry, I'm just nervous. Let's go."

She followed him to the dance floor, only to discover, to her horror, that her mind refused to tell her what to do. She just stood there until finally (in disgust, Amanda was sure), Evan took her hands and placed them on his shoulders. Then he put his own hands on her waist and began to rock back and forth, kind of like a short, wavy-haired robot.

Amanda couldn't wait for the music to be over. But, at the same time, she knew it could have been much worse. Evan didn't try to look at her. And he sort of smelled kind of good. Plus, he was nice enough to pretend not to notice that she was shaking just a little.

Even better, when it was over, the multiplication dance was finished, too. Amanda felt so relieved, she could have hugged Evan right there.

Fortunately, however, he walked off before she could, with a wave and quick, "See ya later."

"That was kind of fun," said Allie, once they'd found each other again. "I mean, after that crazy Jon thing. What was that about, anyway?" She made a face. "Did you see how I looked at him and didn't say a word?" She laughed.

"Yeah," said Amanda, nodding slowly. "Not talking to him, that's definitely the way to go."

"Totally," said Allie. "Oh, and here comes Henley!" She waved up high, over Amanda's shoulder. "*Hen!* Get over here already and tell me about your boyfriend. Have you been keeping him a secret?"

Both Megan and Jen started howling as they followed Henley over. Henley was giggling, too.

"No! No!" she said, shaking her head and waving her hands to emphasize her objection. "That's my cousin, Michael." She laughed again. "He gave me five bucks to dance with him first, so he could ask Melanie Burruss to dance before anyone else did. Apparently, the whole eighth grade has a thing for her."

She reached into her purse and pulled out a folded five-dollar bill. "Aren't cousins great?" she said, grinning. Then she tucked the bill away and grabbed Amanda's and Allie's hands.

"Come on, guys. What are you waiting for? Let's dance! By the way, Mandy," she added. "That skirt is too cute!"

"It really is," agreed Megan.

On a cloud of wardrobe approval, Amanda followed the girls onto the dance floor. At the same time, she wanted to kick herself. *Why couldn't I have been as honest about Jon as Henley just was about her cousin?*

"Hey, Mandy!" Allie yelled over the music, looking concerned. "Are you thinking about Jon?"

Amanda smiled weakly and tried to concentrate a little harder on her dancing. *If she only knew!*

"Don't worry about him," Allie told her. She smiled, took Amanda's hand, and spun her around. "Remember, the best revenge is to look like you're having fun!"

Chapter Nine

DEAR MANDY,

WHERE WERE YOU IN LUNCH? WE MISSED YOU! (I SAT WITH HEN AND MEG AND JENNY. THEY ALL THOUGHT YOUR IMPRESSION OF HAMM DANCING WAS HILARIOUS!)

TOO BAD THERE'S NOT A DANCE EVERY FRIDAY. (WAIT, I TAKE THAT BACK! I'D RUN OUT OF THINGS TO WEAR!) BUT I WAS PSYCHED TO SEE THE NEW SIGNS UP FOR THE TALENT SHOW! OF COURSE WE HAVE TO DO OUR ACT FROM CAMP (ADAPTED FOR OUR NEW AUDIENCE!). I ALREADY SIGNED US UP! LET'S START WORKING ON IT THIS WEEK. WHAT DAYS ARE YOU FREE?

OOPS! CHEESIE-LOUISEE'S STARING AT ME! BETTER START SKETCHING. (HEY, WE SHOULD GET HER AND HAMM TOGETHER — GET IT?)

XXXOOO,
ALLIE

OBTW—I STILL THINK JON WAS TRYING TO MAKE YOU JEALOUS—BUT I TOTALLY GET WHAT YOU SAID THIS WEEKEND ABOUT WANTING TO FORGET HE WAS EVER YOUR BOYFRIEND. (NO MATTER HOW CUTE HE IS AND HOW NICE HE PRETENDS TO BE.) YO COMPRENDE! (ESPAÑOL!)

Amanda folded up the note Allie had handed to her on the way into English. She looked back over her shoulder to give Allie a little smile. But inside, she was *screaming*!

She couldn't believe it! It had taken her most of the weekend to convince Allie that it was best for everyone to just pretend Jon didn't exist. And now, here was another, brand-new problem. It was just like a game of Whac-A-Mole — only it was her life!

The talent show.

Amanda turned to the desk on her left, where Kate usually sat. The bell was just about to ring, but it was still empty — probably because Kate had to drop off her flute in her locker on the other side of school. (Amanda hated having to lug her cello to and from school, but at least she got to leave the beast in the orchestra room during the day.)

Good old Kate, thought Amanda. Kate, who was counting on entering the talent show with Amanda again this year. Kate, who was still trying to process the fact that Amanda had gone to the dance on Friday night without her.

She'd found out at lunch in the music room, where Amanda had suggested they eat their meal — *alone*. The whole point of avoiding the cafeteria had been to keep Kate from finding out. Amanda knew she'd never be able to keep the dance from popping up with Allie at the table, so she'd suggested to Kate that they take their lunches to the music room and get in some extra practice. And that was fine with Kate. Although they'd already played together on Sunday, they now had the talent show to work on, too, and they definitely needed all the practice they could get.

"So, I was thinking," Kate had said, between quick bites of ham and cheese.

Amanda nodded. "I'm listening."

"Well, what would you say," said Kate, "about turning our duo into a trio? I mean, our song sounds great with just us, but don't you think it could sound awesome if we added a violin or something, too?"

"Yeah!" said Amanda, smiling. "That's a great idea. Who were you thinking? Eve?"

Eve was one of their friends from orchestra, and though she could be pretty intense about her music (no doubt because her dad was the conductor of a *real* orchestra, downtown), she always made whatever she played sound really good.

"Kind of." Kate grinned and shrugged. "Who knows, she might even let us rehearse in her dad's studio."

"Then maybe she'll let us hang out in her backyard pool, too," Amanda chimed in. "Do you think it's still open?"

Kate's eyes twinkled. "I hope so!"

"Hi, guys!"

An uninvited face with dimples suddenly appeared at the door.

"I thought I heard people in here. Skipping lunch, huh? Hey, have you seen my backpack, by any chance? I seem to have, uh, misplaced it." The boy laughed.

It was Evan, decent dancer, trumpet player, *and* the boy famous since kindergarten for losing everything.

"Hi, Evan," said Amanda. "Come on in and look around. I haven't seen it, though. How many times does this make for you losing that thing, anyway?" she asked. "A hundred? Or more?"

"Ha-ha," said Evan. "Very funny. As a matter of fact, I've never lost this particular backpack." He grinned. "I just got it last week." Then he got down on his hands and knees and began to scan the floor. "My mom'll kill me if I lose it, though," he muttered.

"Um, is this it?" Kate asked. She held up a dark blue bag by its padded shoulder strap. "It was on You-Know-Who's desk."

"That's it!" said Evan. "What? Are you too much of a lady to say, 'Have enough butts'?" He climbed to his feet and walked over to Kate, smiling. "Thanks," he said.

He took the loose strap in his hand. Then he turned to Amanda. "I'm glad at least one of you two could be helpful," he teased. "And after I was nice enough to ask you to dance."

Amanda could instantly feel her own smile draining away, as if someone had just pulled a plug somewhere deep down in her guts. She cut her eyes to Kate, whose own smile simply seemed to have frozen in place.

Oblivious, Evan went on. "Too bad you weren't there," he told Kate. "Were you? Your friend —" he pointed to Amanda "— was totally out of control! Where did you girls learn to dance, anyway?" He laughed, shook his head, and headed toward the door.

"Thanks again, Kate. *Ave atque Vale,* Amanda! Hail and good-bye!"

Amanda hadn't even had to check to know exactly what Kate looked like. It was the same look Kate had given their third grade teacher when she'd told the class that their pet, Frankenhamster, had died. (Amanda never understood why she didn't just say the poor guy ran away.) The same look she'd given her brother when he'd told her she was adopted. (Not true, by the way.) And the same look she'd given her father when he'd told her she couldn't go to arts camp that summer.

It was not a look, however, that Kate had ever given *her*.

"You went to the dance on Friday?" Kate said — rather pleasantly, considering.

Evan was already long gone, leaving the door wide open behind him.

Amanda looked up slowly, needing as much time as possible to figure out what to say.

"I . . . uh . . . yeah. It just came up, you know . . . at the last minute."

"You just decided, at the last minute, to go?"

"Kind of," said Amanda. She made her way over to the classroom door and closed it. "I mean, well . . . Allie wanted to go."

"But I thought you had some kind of 'stupid stuff' to do or something." Kate crossed her arms and leaned back, waiting for Amanda to respond.

Amanda gulped and tried hard not to wring her hands in desperation. (She knew it would look hopelessly guilty and lame.) But she couldn't help it.

"I did," she blurted. "But it got . . . cancelled. And then, well, Allie wanted to go . . . And I couldn't say no . . . And I totally would have called you, except . . . I thought maybe you'd be practicing and, well . . . I knew you wouldn't want to go."

She looked up into Kate's eyes, which were not *hard,* exactly, but not a bit forgiving, either.

"I mean," Amanda went on meekly, "I knew you didn't want to go, or you would have wanted to do that on Friday instead of practice. Right?"

Kate uncrossed her arms and moved her hands to her hips. "No," she said, "you *didn't* know that I didn't want to go, because you didn't ask me. Last year, you laughed at the idea of going to any school dance. The last thing I thought was that you'd want to go this year . . . especially without me."

"I'm so sorry, Kate," said Amanda. She really, really meant it. "I didn't mean to hurt your feelings. I never thought . . . I never thought you'd find out."

"I know," said Kate dully. "And that's what hurts even more."

She slumped into a chair and flicked the handle on her flute case.

Amanda felt horrible. Horrible for leaving Kate out. Horrible for lying. Horrible for hurting her friend's feelings. She had to make it up to Kate somehow.

"Do you . . . still want to practice?" she asked Kate, sitting down beside her.

"No," said Kate.

And so they just sat there in silence, for twenty full minutes, until orchestra class began.

By the end of the class, however, things were looking up — slightly. Amanda had asked Eve to join their talent show act, and she had happily agreed. She had even asked them to come over to rehearse (and swim!) that afternoon.

It wasn't too late, Amanda reassured herself, to make everything better with Kate. What was it the doctor had told her after she broke her arm in fourth grade? *The place where a bone breaks, then mends, is always stronger.*

And *then* came English, and Allie's tidal wave of a note.

Of course they should redo their act from camp for the talent show. It would be fun. Even *more* fun, Amanda hated to say, than playing her cello. But there was no way she could disappoint Kate — and now Eve, too! — by backing out of the act they'd planned to do. No. Way. Period. Especially not after the whole dance thing!

What was she going to do? How could Amanda say no to Allie, who'd already signed them up? And how could she say no to Kate, whose feelings she'd already bruised?

Could I be in two different acts? she wondered. Doubtful, but she could ask. . . .

In fact, Amanda was just thinking about who to ask when the sixth period bell rang. Kate hurried into English just as Mr. Kleger was about to close the door. Amanda tried to give her a smile, but Kate slid right into her seat, took out a pencil and piece of paper, and quickly began to write.

She finished the note, folded it, and handed it stiffly across the aisle to Amanda.

Amanda opened the note and felt her stomach turn to stone — molten, boiling-over, volcanic, miserable stone.

Just went to sign up for the talent show. Saw Allie and "Mandy" already on it. When were you going to tell me about that? And Eve? Thanks a lot, Amanda.

I hope you and your new best friend are very happy.
Kate

Amanda tried to get Kate's attention to mouth "Wait, you don't understand!" But Kate refused to look her way. She appeared to be concentrating intently on Mr. Kleger's instructions for the day's writing assignment.

Amanda tried to listen, too, but her body was not cooperating. Her outsides were sweaty and her insides were in knots. She would be lucky to make it through the next forty-five minutes without throwing up.

Chapter Ten

From: AllieOop@amerimail.com
To: Hays3@amerimail.com
Sent: Tuesday, September 11, 2007 5:14 PM
Subject: Feeling better?

Hope so. You really lost it there in English yesterday. Did you know the room smelled so bad after you got sick, Eager Kleger let us finish the period outside? (Thanks.) :-0
   You didn't miss much today, I guess. But somebody missed you. Jon came up in homeroom and asked me where you were. You know, I've got to ask you something about him. It can wait till you get back to school though. Tomorrow? I hope.
Allie

OBTW—Ate lunch with Kate today. The three of us should really talk when you get back to school, too.

Oh, no. Amanda had the overwhelming urge to throw up *again*. It wasn't the stomach bug this time, though. That had been gone for hours. It was the feeling that her life was officially over. And she hadn't even turned thirteen yet.

She read Allie's e-mail again and again, line by terrible line. Actually, she skipped the part about her throwing up in English after a while. That, by itself, would have been sufficiently mortifying. But compared to Allie's other news, it was downright amusing.

The parts that really got Amanda were the things she'd missed that day. Things that clearly spelled an end to any and all friendships.

So, Jon had come up and talked to Allie. She could see the conversation right then:

Jon: Hi. Where's your goofy friend? (He probably still didn't know her name.)
Allie: You mean Mandy? Your old girlfriend? She's sick. Didn't you hear she threw up all over English yesterday?
Jon: Oh, yeah. Everyone's talking about that.

But I didn't know that was her name. Because she is NOT MY OLD GIRLFRIEND! If she told you that, she must be a BIG FAT LIAR!

So, of course Allie had to ask her something about Jon. She had to ask Amanda if she really thought she could keep such a major, ridiculous, obvious lie about him a secret!

That's probably why Allie went and sat with Kate at lunch. She wanted to ask Kate if Amanda kept secrets and lied to her "friends" all the time.

Allie: I can't believe it! Guess what Mandy told me? She told me Jon Hopewell was her boyfriend. Seriously! At camp this summer. She lied to me all this time!

Kate: Join the club! She never told me about the back-to-school dance, or that she had signed up to do the talent show with *you*.

Allie: Well, I hate her.

Kate: Yeah, I hate her, too.

Allie and Kate: Let's tell everyone what she did, and then we'll all tell her what a loser she is when she gets back to school!

Well, Amanda wasn't going back to school. Not tomorrow. Not the next day. Not ever.

This wasn't exactly a plan that flew with her mother, however. . . .

"You look fine to me," her mom said, the next morning. She laid her hand on Amanda's forehead and smoothed back her hair. "You don't have a fever. You haven't been sick for a whole day now. I'm sure it's just the twenty-four-hour thing that Dad had." She smiled. "You'll feel much better if you get up and take a shower."

"I don't think so," Amanda replied, as weakly as she could. "I really think I need to stay in bed." She let out a little moan and, closing her eyes, turned wearily away.

Still, she could hear her mother sigh and could easily imagine her gentle expression growing harder.

"You know I *have* to work today, don't you, Amanda?" she said. "I have a closing on a house this morning and several more I'm scheduled to show."

Amanda meekly nodded. "That's okay, Mom," she said wearily. "You can leave me here alone."

"No, Amanda, I cannot. I cannot leave you home alone if you're sick."

Amanda moaned again — this time with good

reason. "I'll be fine, Mom," she said. "Really, you can go."

"Amanda." Her mom put her hand on Amanda's shoulder. Her hair was already fixed, her makeup was applied perfectly, and she was wearing the suit she always wore to her most important meetings. She not only looked very pretty, but very business-like, as well.

"Are you *really* still feeling sick," she asked sternly, "or are you *lying* to me? I need to know." Her tone softened a little. "I mean, I can always reschedule my appointments and get Dad to come home while I'm at the closing, but not just because you don't feel like going to school. Trust me. I know. Pretending to be sick doesn't make school go away." She smiled and took Amanda's hand, which Amanda noticed was nearly the same size as her own. "I also know, hon, that we need to be honest with each other. Now, is there some reason why you don't want to go to school? A test you didn't study for? An assignment you didn't do?"

Amanda pursed her lips and shook her head in silence.

"Well, why don't you lie here for ten more minutes, then get up and have a little breakfast?

Let's see how you're feeling when it's time to leave for school."

When it was time to leave for school, Amanda had eaten three bowls of cereal, two yogurts, and a banana. (She hadn't eaten, after all, in more than a day.) And although she was dreading school more than before, she did not tell her mother.

"Uh-oh, you're late," said her mom, glancing at the clock. "But that's okay. I'll drop you off. Got all your stuff?"

When they got to school, the entrance was deserted and all but one bus had already pulled away. It was so quiet and still, most people wouldn't have guessed the drama about to unfold inside. But the calm facade didn't fool Amanda.

She climbed begrudgingly out of the passenger's seat and weakly shut the door behind her.

"Now, you seem just fine," her mom said as she pulled Amanda's cello out of the trunk. "But if you start to feel sick later, just go to the nurse and have her call me." She handed the heavy case over to Amanda. "I love you, honey. Have a great day!"

Amanda trudged up the steps, lugging her instrument behind her, and pushed through the school's foreboding front doors. The halls were basically empty, the first bell having already rung, and Amanda hurried to drop off her cello in the orchestra room right away.

That done, she debated whether to go to her locker or get to homeroom as soon as possible. But she was already late, and she would need her textbook, so she figured a few more minutes wouldn't hurt.

She headed up the stairs to the second floor, down the gray-and-blue-tiled hallway, past her Latin class, straight toward the third locker on the —

Wait! Who was that? Standing right by the — yes! — the third locker on the right.

Amanda stopped and stared. It was Jon, shaggy hair and all. He was slipping something through the vent in her locker door!

Before she could think of what to do or say next, he had turned and darted through the doors to the opposite stairway, on his way back to homeroom.

Amanda couldn't be sure, but what Jon had put in her locker looked a lot like a note. She could feel her enormous breakfast begin to turn and churn inside her, like cement in a mixer.

She could only imagine the horrible things that awful note must contain:

DEAR LOSER,
HOW DARE YOU SAY I WAS YOUR BOYFRIEND?
I WOULDN'T GO OUT WITH YOU IF YOU WERE THE
LAST GIRL ON EARTH!
JUST WHO DO YOU THINK YOU ARE? (WHATEVER YOUR
NAME IS.)

And with a sinking feeling as big as the *Titanic* (no lie!), Amanda realized that she didn't just have Kate and Allie to worry about. She had Jon and probably everyone else in the whole school to fear now, too.

But before she could cross the thirty miserable steps to her miserable locker and read the miserable note for her miserable self, the door of the Latin room burst open. Mrs. Blau blew out, swinging a purse the size of a duffel bag over her broad, bony shoulder.

"Amanda! *Salve!* Hello, there. What are you doing up here? You were supposed to meet me down by the bus, remember?"

Amanda knew she looked puzzled, but then she suddenly remembered. It was Wednesday. Of course! The day of the Latin field trip. She'd completely forgotten about it!

"Right, Mrs. Blau — I mean, *Magistra*," she said.

"I remember. Let me just go to my locker, and I'll be right there."

"Oh, no, no, no!" yelped the teacher. "No time! *Ex vicis!*" She quickly moved between Amanda and her locker and began to herd her down the hall, like a runaway sheep. "We've got a lot to see and —" She checked her watch. "I think we're late already. It's fine if you bring your backpack. You have a pencil and paper in there, I hope." She grabbed Amanda's hand. "Good. Come with me."

Amanda had no choice. She looked wistfully back at her locker as Mrs. Blau whisked her down the hall. The note would have to wait, it seemed.

They emerged through the front doors to find a dozen waiting students — both seventh and eighth graders — sitting on the steps. The bus Amanda had seen before was at the curb, and as Mrs. Blau descended the steps, the yellow door folded open with a weary, uninspired hiss.

"*Salvete, Discipuli,*" said the teacher. "Sorry to keep you waiting. *Ave!* We have a lot of buildings to see — and not much time if we're to return before lunch!"

Mrs. Blau leaped onto the bus and the students followed, one by one. Amanda would have been happy to be the last in line, but Evan stood and politely waved her ahead.

"Ladies first," he said, grinning.

"Thanks," Amanda mumbled.

"Hey, Mandy!"

Amanda turned, to see Henley running over from a white car near the steps.

"Hi," said Amanda. She grinned, completely forgetting for a moment that Henley might know everything about her lies and secrets, too.

"Missed the bus," Henley said, nodding. She didn't seem to be acting any differently than usual. "Where are you going?" she asked with a curious smile.

Amanda relaxed. "Latin field trip."

"Cool," said Henley. She ran up the steps, then paused and turned around. "Have fun," she called down to Amanda. "Hey, will you be back for lunch?"

Amanda sighed, both with relief that Henley didn't seem aware of her *situation* and with acceptance of the fact that she would, indeed, be returning to school.

"Yeah, I think so," she called back. "Bye, Henley," she said, waving.

"Yeah, bye, Henley," Evan echoed.

Henley, who'd just reached the school door, stopped and turned in surprise.

"Oh, hey . . ." She smiled and raised her hand halfway. "Evan, right? See ya. Bye."

"So tell me . . . does she have a boyfriend?" Evan asked as Amanda stepped onto the bus.

"Oh, Evan." Amanda sighed. She shook her head as she climbed the steps and dragged herself down the narrow aisle. He was nice and all, but did he really think he stood a chance? Plus, Amanda had her own problems, and wanted nothing more than to scrunch down in the backseat of the bus and hide.

"Oh, no, no, Amanda, darling." Mrs. Blau waved to her from the front. "Don't sit back there. You might not be able to hear me. Come. *Venis.* Sit over here by Evan." She pointed to the second seat behind the driver.

With a sigh, Amanda reversed her direction. Evan sat down and smiled as she slid in beside him.

"There'll be no napping on this bus ride," he joked.

"I guess not," muttered Amanda.

"So . . . does she? Have a boyfriend?"

In front of them, the driver put the bus in gear and allowed it to lurch away from the school with a rusty growl.

Amanda braced herself with her arm. "No," she said flatly. "No, she does not."

"Sweet." Evan pumped his fist in the air, then grinned bashfully at Amanda. "A guy can dream, can't he?"

Amanda rolled her eyes, though she couldn't help but smile.

"Hey, where were you yesterday?" he went on. He slid down and propped his knees on the back of the seat in front of them.

"Sick," she replied, staring stiffly ahead. Then she shot him a dubious look out of the corner of her eye. "I threw up in English on Monday. Didn't you hear?"

"Oh, right!" He laughed. "I did! I heard they had to leave the windows open overnight. Green puke everywhere! Way to go!"

"Actually," she said solemnly, "it was more brownish. And it was quite contained. But thank you." She turned to him, smiling this time, and bowed her head dramatically.

"Maybe you should eat what they serve in the cafeteria instead of in the music room from now on," he told her.

"Yeah," she agreed, her smile fading away. "Maybe I should."

She looked past Evan, out the window at the smaller cars cheerfully whizzing by. They'd already left the leafy side streets of the suburbs behind and were now hurtling down the highway toward the city. To her, the city always meant her dad's store — and the Japanese steakhouse she loved to go to on her birthday.

"I didn't, uh, miss anything yesterday, did I?" she cautiously inquired. She didn't really think Evan would have talked much to Kate, Allie, *or* Jon. But she had to ask.

He thought for a minute. "No." He shrugged. "I don't think so. Blau prepped us for the field trip, of course. She showed us how to make a rubbing. Oh, shoot!" He slapped his forehead. "I think I forgot paper. Do you have some I could borrow?"

Amanda nodded and patted her backpack. "I have tons."

"Cool," said Evan. "Thanks." Then he winced. "How 'bout something to write on?"

Amanda rolled her eyes. "No problem," she told him. "Do you need a pencil, too?"

"No," he said, looking insulted. Then he paused. "Oh, wait. Actually, I do."

Amanda shook her head and looked out the window again. They were just passing Amanda's dad's store. She would have liked to have waved to him, but the gate was still down. There was still a half hour until the store opened, and if she knew her dad, he was probably down the street at the Main Street Café, reading the paper and having his fifth or sixth cup of coffee.

"Hey, Hays Shoes!" exclaimed Evan. "I forgot I was sitting by the Shoe Queen. All hail the Queen of Shoes!"

"Shoe *Princess*," Amanda corrected him in her most haughty, royal tone. "I'm just the heir. I'm not on the throne yet."

"Oh, that reminds me," Evan said. "We got new music in orchestra yesterday, too. 'The Coronation March.'" He winked and gave a thumbs-up. "It's got a trumpet solo."

"Cool." Amanda nodded.

"I'm thinking maybe I'll do it for the talent show," he went on. "Are you and Kate going to play something again this year?"

Amanda's mood, which had been rising, suddenly took a dive. "I don't know," she said stiffly.

"Oh," Evan replied.

She could tell that he wasn't sure what he'd said to offend her. But she was in no mood at all to explain.

"Well, you guys were good last year," he said, turning back to the window. "If you ask me, you should."

Just then a squeal filled the air as the whole bus reeled forward, then grunted to a stop in front of City Hall and the Courthouse.

"Okay, class. We're here!" Mrs. Blau rose to her feet and waved her hands above her head. "*Ave, Discipuli!* This way!" She bounded out onto the sidewalk, both hands still flapping in the air.

Amanda looked at Evan. Regardless of her troubled mood, there was no way she could resist.

"Well, you heard her," she said, raising her hands over her head. "This way!" And she followed Mrs. Blau out of the bus, waving her hands in just the same way. Evan followed behind, cracking up.

The teacher didn't seem to notice, however. She was far too excited about the activity at hand and was already attacking the steps of the Courthouse, two — even three — at a time.

"Now," Mrs. Blau declared as her students assembled before her, "I know many people regard Latin as a *dead* language. 'Why do we need it?' they ask. 'It hasn't been spoken for hundreds of years.'" She looked at them eagerly, undeterred by the sea of blank, blurry faces. "But Latin is *very* much alive in the arts, science, law — and, as you Harry Potter fans know, *magic.*"

"'*Expecto Patronum!*'" shouted Evan.

"Er . . . yes, *exactly,*" said Mrs. Blau. "Anyway, that's what brings us here today. Many of you probably haven't even noticed the Latin words and phrases that adorn our most-revered buildings. On the walls of both the Courthouse and City Hall are Latin mottos that our community strives to live by. Your mission, should you choose to accept it, and" — she grinned — "I recommend that you do, is to find a motto that speaks to you, and make a rubbing of it. *Ave, Discipuli!* This way!"

It was actually pretty amazing, Amanda realized as they walked around the square. She'd never noticed all the Latin words inscribed on the government buildings.

"'IUSTITIA OMNIBUS,'" Mrs. Blau read off the wall of the courthouse. "Who can tell me what that means? Anyone . . ."

"You should *sit* on the bus?" suggested an eighth grader with glasses.

"No." Mrs. Blau smiled. "*Iustitia,* justice; *omnis,* all. 'Justice for all.' And how about this one?" She pointed to the carved marble pediment over the door. "Theo? Would you read it, please?"

A tall boy spoke up. "Vincent . . . omnya . . . ver?"

"Um, no, Theo. Excuse me." Mrs. Blau held up her hand. "Remember your pronunciation. 'VINCIT OMNIA VERITAS.' 'WIN-keet' — not Vincent —

means 'conquer.' 'OM-nee-uh' — all, or 'everyone.' And 'WEAR-i-tas.' That's 'truth.' 'Truth conquers all.'"

"Hey, Mrs. Blau, here's another 'Weird-eat-us' over here," called Evan, who'd wandered over to one of two bubbling fountains. He pointed to three words carved in its marble base. "What does this one mean?"

"Ah, 'VERITAS LUX MEA.' The truth is my *lux,* or 'light.' That's a lovely one!" said Mrs. Blau. "I believe there's another one on the other fountain as well. Amanda, would you go over and read it for us?"

Amanda walked over to the other fountain and tried her best to sound out the awkward words: "WEAR-i-tas . . . vos . . . LEE-ber-ah-bit."

"Lee-ber-AH-bit. Very nice, Amanda." Mrs. Blau smiled. "And there is that word *veritas* yet again!"

Yes. Amanda couldn't help but notice. *Veritas.* Truth. *There it is again. . . .*

"*Liberabit,*" said a girl named Mia. "That sounds a little like 'liberty,' and a little like 'rabbit.'"

"Free the rabbit!" howled two eighth-grade boys.

"Now, now, boys," said Mrs. Blau, rubbing her head. "Actually, the 'free' part is absolutely right. *Libero* means 'to free.' 'The truth will set you free!'"

Veritas vos liberabit, thought Amanda. *The truth will set you free.*

Mrs. Blau showed them several more mottos, but this one stuck like gum on the sidewalk of Amanda's brain.

The truth will set you free.

The truth will *set me free!* she realized. It was a sign. A sign from the Roman gods!

She had no doubt at all which motto she would be taking home. *Enough lies!* Amanda thought as she opened up her backpack. *Veritas vos liberabit!*

Chapter Eleven

MEET US IN THE MUSIC ROOM!

The note wasn't signed. But by now, Amanda knew the handwriting as well as her own. What it *meant*, though, she didn't know. And she wasn't so sure she wanted to find out.

She'd gotten the note from Henley just as she entered the cafeteria after the field trip. She'd been dying to find Allie, and then Kate, and bare her guilty soul. But neither Allie nor Kate was anywhere to be found.

She'd stopped to wonder if maybe they, too, had gotten sick and were now home staring into their respective toilets when Henley suddenly shouted her name.

"Hey, Mandy! How was the field trip?" she asked.

"Uh, good. I mean, if you can take Mrs. Blau's *enthusiasm*." Amanda pumped her arms. *"Ave, Discipuli!"*

"Oh, that's funny!" Henley giggled. "Hey, I have something for you." She pulled a square of folded paper from her purse and handed it to Amanda. "I told Allie I saw you this morning and that you were back in school, and she wanted me to give you this if I saw you. So, here you are." She held out her hand. "And here it is!"

Amanda took the note, opened it, and read the six ominous words.

"Is something wrong?" Henley asked her. "Allie seemed good. Is everything okay?"

"Oh, no." Amanda tried to work her fallen face into a less tragic expression. "Everything's fine, but I, uh . . ." She swallowed hard. "I guess I have to go."

"Oh," said Henley. She pouted. "Too bad. We'll see you later." Then she turned back to the table. "So anyway, yes, he's kind of cute. . . ."

Amanda trudged away, wishing she could have stayed to hear more about some cute boy, and wishing she didn't have to face Allie *this* way. Clearly, Allie was furious with her. Much madder than Amanda had imagined, if this note was any indication. She'd never even seen Allie mad before, she realized — and she was suddenly afraid.

She wasn't just scared of Allie, either. There was a "we" waiting for her. Without a doubt, it was the same "we" that Allie had said really needed to talk to Amanda in yesterday's e-mail.

Yes, she'd wanted to come clean to Allie and Kate — but not *together*! Not this way!

And what if, horror of horrors, the "we" also included Jon?

Jon? she thought, with a sinking feeling that actually made her groan out loud. Was the note in her locker not enough?

The note in her locker!

She'd been so eager to get to lunch and see Allie, she'd completely forgotten to see what Jon had left for her. Not that she *really* wanted to read it. But should she go get it right now? Her locker was way on the other side of the school, and there wasn't that much time left in the period at all. . . .

No, she was nearly to the music room; she might as well face the music then and there. The note could wait.

Amanda walked up to the music room door and reached for the handle. . . .

"Stop!" she cried out as soon as she pushed the door open. "Stop! What's going on!"

.What was going on was that Allie was sitting on a desk, pretending to play the flute, and Kate was shrieking and pawing at her, trying to grab it back.

"What are you doing?" Amanda shouted. Though she was really thinking, *What have I done?*

Kate let go of the flute and quickly spun around, while Allie jumped off the desk and looked up, surprised.

"Hey! You got our note! How was the field trip?"

"Feeling better, I hope?" Kate chimed in.

Amanda paused to catch her breath. "You guys have to stop fighting," she panted. "You have every right to be mad at me, but please don't hate each other!"

Kate and Allie stared at Amanda, then turned slowly to one another.

"Do you hate me?" asked Allie.

"No," said Kate. "Do you hate me?"

"Uh, no!" Allie wrinkled her forehead in mock confusion, then both girls grinned and shared a laugh.

"What?" said Amanda. "So . . . you're not mad at each other?"

"No!" said Allie and Kate together, as one.

Amanda sighed. "Well, that's good, at least."

"And we're not mad at you, either," said Kate. She blew a big pink bubble, let it pop, and sucked the gum back in.

"No?" It was Amanda's turn to crease her forehead. "I thought — I thought you were."

Allie smacked her own gum and shrugged her shoulders. "About what?"

"Well," Amanda sighed. *Where to begin?* "About the talent show, for one thing," she said, turning to Kate. "You sure were mad at me on Monday."

Kate bit her lip and nodded. "Yeah, I was. But," she added, smiling, "that was before Allie and I talked yesterday."

"Right," said Allie. "I saw Kate the Great here, sitting alone in lunch yesterday, so I went over, and we started talking. I asked her about the talent show and if she was planning to do anything —"

"And I didn't have an answer," Kate cut in.

"Right." Allie grinned. "So I said, 'Well, I just signed Mandy and me up — why don't you do something with us?' I mean, I knew she played an instrument, and it suddenly hit me: That's exactly what our skit needs!"

Amanda was completely stunned.

"Don't you think?" Allie went on.

Amanda nodded. "Uh, yeah, yeah, I do. But . . ." She hesitated. "What exactly are you thinking? And, um," She turned to Kate. "What about Eve?"

"Oh, she can be in it, too," said Allie. "I mean, I hope so. She's absent today. But our beauty contestants need talents, don't they? And only one can play the cello, and there's only so much singing and dancing the two of us can do." She threw her hands in the air. "So I was thinking, what if we got Kate and Eve both to play?"

"I don't want to *act* in it, though," Kate added quickly.

"Right," Allie said. "So she's going to play off-stage, and I'll pretend to do the playing." She raised Kate's flute and merrily fluttered her fingers. "I've always wanted to play the flute, you know!"

"I can play background music, too." Kate went on, happily. "Like when you guys are modeling. And when the winner gets crowned."

Allie looked at Amanda, beaming. "It's going to take this thing to a whole new level, don't you think?"

Amanda felt like two tons had been lifted off her back. "I think it sounds awesome!" Why hadn't *she* thought of that?

It was perfect. It was wonderful. It was going to turn out great. And best of all, it meant her two best friends didn't hate her — or each other — after all.

"This is great!" said Amanda, giving Allie a grateful hug. "And thank you so much for not being mad about my lie!"

Allie stood back and gave Amanda a sideways, puzzled look. "What lie?" she asked.

Amanda could feel her face get hot as her blood pumped faster. And faster. "Um . . . about . . . Jon?"

"What about him?" Allie asked.

What about him? Allie's question echoed through Amanda's mind. Could it be? Was it possible? Allie still didn't know?

"Uh . . ." There was a tiny voice inside her urging Amanda to say, *Never mind.* But the answer tumbled out anyway, completely on its own: "That he was my boyfriend." She tried to read Allie's blank face. Could she really not have known?

Allie remained silent. But Kate immediately started to howl.

"You told her *what?*" said Kate. "Ha, ha, *ha!*" She laughed and doubled over.

Amanda, however, was concentrating on Allie. It looked as if a million thoughts were racing through her mind, and Amanda wondered how many of them involved her and various forms of torture.

At last, Allie spoke. "So, he was *never* your boyfriend?"

Amanda slowly shook her head. "Never," she confessed carefully. "But I thought you knew! I mean, I really thought from your e-mail yesterday . . . I don't know. You said you had to ask me something about him. You said he'd come up to you in homeroom. And I just — I just figured you'd found out I'd been lying. And . . ." She put her hands together, just like a bad actress in a play. (Maybe, come to think of it, they weren't so bad after all.) "I am so, *so* sorry!

"I didn't mean to lie to you," she went on. "I just thought . . . you seemed to think it was so cool at camp, and I guess I did, too. I thought what did it matter, no one would find out. And then you *moved* here, and then I thought you wouldn't want to be my friend anymore if I told you the truth, and then I hoped it would just go away, and then it never did, and then I felt so guilty, and —" She stopped to gasp for air. "And I promise, Allie. I'll never lie to you again. You, too," she added, glancing in Kate's direction, "if you'll *please* just stop *laughing*!"

Kate respectfully bit her lip, while Allie silently took a seat.

"So, wait," Allie said after a moment. She cocked her head. "Are you saying Jon hasn't really been ignoring you all this time?"

"No!" said Amanda. "That's the thing! He hardly even knows me."

"So he really isn't a total jerk?"

"No!" said Amanda. "Not at *all.*"

Amanda watched as Allie processed this late-breaking piece of news. She really wished that Allie would just *say* something. She wished she'd yell at her and get it over with, already. She wished she'd tell Amanda how she could, hopefully, make it up to her. *Or,* she thought as her heart sank like lead, *not.*

"Well," said Amanda, finally, when she couldn't take it any longer. "Do you hate me now?"

Allie shook her head. "No, Mandy," she said. "I don't hate you."

"No?" said Amanda, a relieved smile beginning to inch across her face.

"No." Allie shook her head. "I mean, I'm the one who saw that picture and instantly turned him into your boyfriend. I remember — *completely.* Of course, you didn't have to go on about *every-thing* you guys had done together and how *much* he liked you. But," she said, smiling, "I can't say I really blame you."

She leaned in and, smiling slyly, looked from Amanda to Kate. "Do you guys *really* want to know a secret?"

Amanda and Kate nodded and leaned forward themselves.

"I think," said Allie, nibbling on a glittery blue fingernail, "I wanted him to be your boyfriend, Mandy, because *I* thought he was so cute. I don't know." She shook her head. "I mean, I *know* he's goofy. But from the minute I saw that picture, I just had the biggest crush." She shrugged and started to blush. "And I still do. And that's what I'd wanted to talk to you about, Mandy. I was feeling so guilty because no matter how hard I tried, I couldn't help liking him. But how uncool is that, crushing on my best friend's ex — and in a brand-new school?

"I'm just *so* glad," Allie went on, "to know he's really not a jerk. I did think it was awful the way he just ignored you." She shook her head. Then she took Amanda's hand and stared at it, puzzled, for a moment.

"So . . . where did this come from?" she asked, pointing to Amanda's silver ring. "Don't tell me you have some *other* boyfriend you've been keeping a secret!"

Kate burst into hysterical laughter once again, and Amanda pointed to her with a sigh.

126

"Uh, no," she said. "This would be a gift from my not-secret best friend over there, Kate the Great, who I *really* wish would stop laughing." She tried to glare at Kate. "She brought it back to me from Ireland."

"Seriously!" Kate gasped, clutching her side. "I can't help it. I'm trying to stop. I am!"

Amanda looked at Allie and was relieved to see that she had started to giggle, too.

"Oh, fine," Amanda said, linking her elbow with Kate's. "So," she added hopefully. "We're all good? Still best friends?"

Allie got up and put her arms around them both. "Totally!" she said. "And I can crush on Jon all I like! Hey," she said suddenly, as a new thought crossed her mind. "Jon's name — did he even change it?"

"Um, I don't think so," Amanda said sheepishly.

"Cool." Allie grinned, and Amanda did, too.

And that's when it hit her.

Jon!

She had completely forgotten about his note!

If Allie hadn't told Jon about her lie, and if Jon wasn't furious with Amanda, then *why* had he slipped something into her locker that morning? What *was* it? And *what* did it say?

Chapter Twelve

DEAR MANDY,

I KNOW I DON'T KNOW YOU THAT WELL, BUT SINCE
YOU'RE ALLIE'S BEST FRIEND, I WAS HOPING YOU COULD
TELL HER THAT I'M NOT AS BIG OF A JERK AS SHE SEEMS
TO THINK I AM. SHE ALWAYS SEEMS MAD AT ME FOR
SOMETHING. DO YOU KNOW WHAT IT IS? IF YOU COULD
TELL ME WHAT IT IS AND TELL HER THAT I DIDN'T MEAN IT,
I'D REALLY APPRECIATE IT. AND COULD YOU ALSO TELL
ME — DOES SHE HAVE A BOYFRIEND FROM HER OLD SCHOOL?
THIS IS REALLY EMBARRASSING, BUT I KIND OF LIKE HER
AND WOULD REALLY LIKE TO KNOW.

PLEASE WRITE ME BACK AND TELL ME IF I HAVE A
CHANCE.

MY LOCKER # IS E254.

THANKS,

JON

Allie was sighing nervously and looking away as Amanda silently read the note.

"I knew it," Allie said, shaking her head sadly. "You may not like him, Mandy, but he's totally liked you from the very first day of school." She shrugged. "It's fine, though, I guess. I mean, now that I've totally ruined my chances by being so mean to him all this time. I'm sure he thinks I'm the biggest jerk in the world." As she spoke, Allie's miserable frown became more of a cool glare. "Thanks to *you*, by the way," she added.

Amanda looked up from the note, wholly incapable of hiding her smile. "Well," she said, brightly, "please allow me make it up to you." She slipped the piece of notebook paper into Allie's hand.

Allie looked down and read the note, her face growing brighter with each word. Her mouth began to tremble, and by the time Allie was finished, Amanda could feel the rest of her shaking, too.

"Oh. My. Gosh!" squealed Kate, who'd been reading over Allie's shoulder. "He likes *you*!"

Allie looked up, smacked her gum, then read the note again.

"I can't believe it," she said. She clutched the note to her chest. "Is it some kind of joke, do you think?"

Amanda shook her head. "I don't think so. Do you, Kate?"

Kate shook her head even harder. "Definitely not," she said.

Around them, the hall was filling steadily with students, either coming from lunch or from their fourth period classes. All three girls glanced around quickly to make sure Jon was nowhere nearby. The coast was clear.

"So what do I *do*?" asked Allie, barely able to contain herself. "What do I say? What happens next? Should I ask him to go out with me, do you think?"

Amanda held up her hands to stop her. "*You* don't do anything," she said. Then she pointed to the note still clenched in Allie's hand. "I should write back to him, just like he says."

"Yeah," Kate agreed. "You should definitely let Amanda — Mandy — write him back. It's much cooler."

"And what are you going to say?" asked Allie.

Amanda grinned. "Well, I'll tell him he *does* have a chance, *maybe*."

"*Grrr!*" Allie shot back with a playful glare. "Come on, be serious!"

"Okay." Amanda laughed. "I'll write something good, don't worry. The bell's going to ring any second, though. So Kate and I will write the note in orchestra, and we'll meet back here before English, okay?"

Allie nodded. "Okay — though I don't think I can wait!" She looked down at the note once more, then clutched it to her chest.

"Hang on," said Amanda. "Where did he say his locker was again?"

Allie looked down. "E254."

"That's on the second floor," said Kate "Maybe we should meet near there."

"Yeah," Amanda agreed. "In the girls' bathroom. By the stairs. Okay, Allie? End of next period. See you there!"

"So, where is it? Let me see!" said Allie breathlessly when they regrouped in the bathroom, fifty minutes later, as planned.

"Gosh! Give me a second," Amanda teasingly replied. She reached into her purse and took out a carefully folded note. "Kate helped me," she said as she handed it to Allie. "What do you think?"

Allie started to open the note just as a bunch of eighth graders came in, giggling and pulling out all sorts of makeup.

"Come on," Allie mumbled. She grabbed Kate and Amanda by the elbows and quickly dragged them into the handicapped stall.

There, they huddled around the note as Allie unfolded it and read:

Dear Jon,
Don't worry about Allie. I checked and she does <u>not</u> think you're a jerk and she is definitely <u>not</u> mad at you. She can just be a little shy — especially around boys.

"Ha!" Allie looked up at Amanda and they shared a knowing smile.

"Well," said Amanda defensively. "I didn't say you *were* a little shy, I said you *can* be a little shy!"

Allie laughed and read on:

And no, she does not have a boyfriend from her old school, either. I bet she would be happy if you e-mailed her tonight. Here is her address:
AllieOop@amerimail.com
Your friend,
Mandy

"So," said Amanda, looking eagerly at Allie. "Does it sound okay?"

"I think it's good," Kate said. "It's totally encouraging, without being too apologetic or too ... desperate, you know?"

Allie nodded. "Yeah, it's good." She smiled and scanned the note once more, then looked thoughtful for a moment. "It just needs one more thing, I think."

She reached into her purse and pulled out a well-chewed pencil. Then she held the note against the wall of the stall (just above a crude, but recognizable, drawing of Señora Barry on a broom with the words, LA BRUJA written below), and prepared to write.

"Hold it!" said Amanda, grabbing Allie's hand. "What are you doing?"

"I just want to write one thing," said Allie.

"Well, you can't!" said Amanda.

"It would look *weird*," Kate told her. "Your handwriting's totally different."

"Oh, right," said Allie. "Well, here." She handed Amanda the pencil and moved back to give her space. "Are you ready?"

"Ready," said Amanda.

"Take this down." Allie took a deep breath and grinned. "OBTW — Allie wanted me to tell you she thinks you're really cute."

A minute later, Amanda, Allie, and Kate burst out of the stall to find the eighth graders still trading lip gloss and staring at them as if they were exchange students from another planet.

"What?" said Amanda as they walked out the

door. She turned to her friends. "Haven't they ever seen people use the stalls before?"

They emerged from the bathroom and headed toward the E200 row of lockers.

There were kids everywhere, walking and running, struggling to yank open their lockers, and slamming them shut with a chorus of *bang* after *bang, bang, BANG.*

The girls scanned the hall for Jon immediately, but thankfully, he seemed to be the one person not around.

Amanda suddenly turned to Allie. "You should stay here," she said. "In case Jon comes by, you know?"

Allie nodded. "You're right. I will," she said. "But *hurry!*"

Amanda could feel Allie's eyes on her back, watching, as she zoomed down the row of lockers with Kate close by her side. They passed the E220s, 230s, and so on, until together they stopped in the middle of the row.

"Is this it?" Kate asked, pointing discreetly as Amanda pulled out the note.

"Yep. And here it goes!"

Quickly, Amanda slid the note through the highest slat of the locker, and listened with satisfaction.

It landed with a whisper on whatever typical boy-mess lay waiting for it inside.

She grinned, just imagining Jon's reaction when he read it, and the whirlwind romance that was sure to follow. She sighed with satisfaction — then jumped at the sound of her name.

"Hey, Amanda. Hey, Kate. What's up?"

Amanda turned. "What? Oh, hi . . . Evan."

Evan studied her suspiciously. "And just what do you think you're doing to my locker?" he asked, crossing his arms.

"*Your* locker?" said Amanda, turning wide-eyed to Kate. Then she spun her head to check the etched number on the door.

E245

Jon's locker was E2*5*4!

Help! Amanda began screaming inside. She turned back to Evan and tried to think of what to say.

"You're never going to believe this, Evan," she finally blurted, "but . . ."

But what *exactly?* she asked herself. *But we accidentally dropped something — of absolutely no interest to you at all — in your locker. Could we have it back? Or better yet: We have reason to believe there has been a curse put on your locker and we highly recommend you never open it again.*

Then Kate stepped up. "Actually, Evan," she said, "we're delivering a note for a friend and we thought this was someone else's locker." She laughed apologetically. "Would you mind terribly getting it for us? It's *very* personal. Very secret," she added. "If we mess this up, our friend will kill us!"

Evan shook his head. "Yeah, I bet!" he said. Then he stepped up and began to dial his combination.

Amanda, meanwhile, flashed Kate a look that clearly said, *You crazy fool!*

Are you kidding? she was thinking. Now that Evan knew it was a "very personal, very secret" note, he was so *totally* going to read it!

She watched with dread as he lined up the final number, then pulled the handle on the door. It swung open and there, perched on what appeared to be Evan's trumpet case and a week and a half's worth of old, crumpled lunch bags, sat the crisp, precious note — a little lamb at the mercy of a hungry wolf.

Amanda moved in to grab it, but Evan beat her to it.

"Oh, Evan," said Amanda, hanging her head. *"Please."*

"Please what?" he said. He handed Kate the

note, still folded in its tight square. "Did you think I would read it or something? Man, I like to joke around, but I'm not a total jerk." He frowned as he grabbed two books from the top shelf, then held the locker door open. "You guys drop anything else in here?" he asked. "Tell me quick. I'm gonna be late if I don't hurry."

"No, but thanks a lot," said Kate. "And don't worry about Amanda." She flashed her a weary look. "She's got *trust* issues. See you in science."

"See ya," Evan told her. "Later, Amanda." Then he slammed his locker and headed toward the stairs.

Kate handed Amanda the note as they watched him walk away. On her face was the slightest of satisfied smirks.

"Sorry," said Amanda. "I mean, I just never thought he'd hand something so private and potentially embarrassing right over."

"You really underestimate people sometimes," Kate told her. "And besides, didn't anyone ever tell you that 'honesty is the best policy'?"

"Obviously not," said Amanda. She looked down at the note. "But I sure have learned my lesson today."

Around them, the crowd in the hall was quickly thinning out. Amanda knew they only had about a minute to drop the note in the right locker and get to English class on time. She linked her elbow with Kate's and pulled her along, past lockers E246 through E253, to the one marked E254.

She stopped and checked the number, one more time. Then she pushed the note through the top slot and ran back to collect Allie.

"What happened back there?" Allie demanded.

Kate laughed, and Amanda simply grabbed them both by the hands.

"Minor difficulties," she said as she ran, dragging her friends with her down the hall. "But don't worry. Right, Kate? Mission accomplished!"

"Girls!" Mrs. Klee's shrill voice rose up behind them. "How many times do I have to tell you: There is no running in the halls!"

Chapter Thirteen

From: AllieOop@amerimail.com
To: Hays3@amerimail.com
Sent: Saturday, October 6, 2007 10:41
Subject: GOOD MORNING!

Hey, hey, Hays! Are you up yet, sleepyhead? ;)
Want to go to the movies this afternoon with
me and Jon? Opening weekend!
Let me know!
CUL8R!
YBFF,
Allie
OBTW—We SO should have won the talent show last
night. Anyone can do a cartwheel! :p Oh, well.
Next year!

Allie was right, thought Amanda. They totally should have won! Their act had come together unbelievably well (if she did say so herself), helped in part by the addition of yet another member to their cast.

It had been Amanda's idea. It had come to her in Latin, on the same day as the field trip and the Locker Note Fiasco, as she neatly traced a border around her courthouse rubbing.

VERITAS VOS LIBERABIT

The truth will set you free.

How true those words had turned out to be. Amanda felt freer and more at ease than she had for *weeks*. And she was so excited for Allie!

But she still felt bad about one thing.

She looked up at the dark, curly head just in front of her. He was funny. He played an instrument. He was easy to be around.

"Hey, Evan," she said, tapping him lightly on the shoulder.

"Yeah?" He turned around.

"I just, um, wanted to say I'm sorry for not trusting you with that note before."

"Whatever." He shrugged. "It's okay."

"Really?" Amanda said.

"Yeah. I mean, we're friends. It's cool."

Amanda smiled with relief.

140

"Evan? Amanda? *Silentium*. Silence, please."

"Yes, *Magistra*," they answered, looking down and laughing.

"Hey, Evan," Amanda whispered after he'd turned back around.

"Hey, what," he whispered back, over his shoulder.

"I was just thinking . . . any interest in doing a talent show skit with Kate, and Allie, and maybe Eve, and me?"

Evan stopped writing and turned around.

"Maybe," he said. "Tell me more about it after school." Then he grinned. "By the way, how'd the note thing turn out?"

"Don't know yet," Amanda whispered, ducking out of Mrs. Blau's view.

In fact, Jon got the note and e-mailed Allie that very afternoon, and Allie called Amanda the minute it came through.

"Listen to this, Mandy!" she said. " *'Allie, I hope it's okay I'm writing you. Mandy gave me your e-mail address. I just wanted to say hi. It's been hard to talk to you at school. How do you like GW? Do you like football? How did you do on the history quiz? Did you get that one for extra credit at the end? CU, Jon'*

"Can you believe it?" said Allie breathlessly. "What do you think?"

141

"I think you have to write him back!" said Amanda.

"Oh, I have!" Allie said. "I haven't sent it yet, though. Here it is: *'Hi, Jon! Of course it's okay if you write me! I've been wanting to talk to you, too! I said "false" on the extra credit. George Washington didn't really cut down a cherry tree.'* He didn't, did he? *'And I LOVE football! There's a game on Friday after school. Are you planning to go? Maybe we could go together. Go Generals! Let me know, Allie. OBTW — Feel free to call me, too.'* And I give him my number. Sound okay to you?"

"Sounds great!" said Amanda.

"And how do think I should sign off?" Allie asked. " 'CU,' like he does? Or 'your friend'? Or just 'Allie'?"

"How 'bout 'CU2'?" said Amanda.

"Perfect!" replied Allie. " 'CU2,' Send!"

"Now," said Amanda playfully, "are you still going to have time to do the talent show — and have a boyfriend?"

"Hey! He's not my boyfriend yet," said Allie. "But of course I will! Are you kidding?"

"Good!" said Amanda. "And I had an idea. Do you know Evan? He's in my Latin class and orchestra. He's the one" — Amanda cleared her throat — "um . . . whose locker I accidentally put Jon's note in."

142

"Oh, yeah!" said Allie.

"Well," Amanda went on. "He's really pretty funny. And very nice, as you know. And I was thinking maybe he should be in our skit, too. He does a mean Mrs. Blau."

"That's a great idea," said Allie. "Which instrument does he play?"

"The trumpet," said Amanda. "In fact, he's learning this one solo that would be perfect at the end, where the winner gets crowned."

"Awesome," said Allie. "Does he have lunch fourth period, too? Or we could all just start getting together after school. That would probably be best, don't you — Oh my gosh!"

Allie screamed so loud, Amanda had to pull the phone away from her ear.

"That's my call waiting!" Allie went on. "I think it's Jon! I have to go!"

Amanda smiled and hung up. *Well, that didn't take long,* she thought. Now to call Kate and share all the news!

And so, by talent show time, two things had happened: *Mandy* (as she'd come to officially be called), Allie, Kate the Great, Eve, and Evan had what they were sure would be the funniest skit in GW history down cold, and Allie and Jon had officially become a couple. In addition, more than a few misconceptions about Jon had been corrected. He was not an Eagle Scout, as Amanda had "imagined" (and Allie was not a bit surprised). He did not play the guitar, though he could play "Boulevard of Broken Dreams" on the harmonica. And his birthday *was* on the seventh . . . of November.

"He's a Scorpio!" said Allie. "Cool!"

Bottom line, he was not the perfect boyfriend Mandy had constructed — but he was just right for Allie, and that was what mattered.

Plus, he was one of their loudest fans at the talent show — not including Kate's little brother and Mandy's mom.

Unfortunately, a squad of eighth grade cheerleaders somersaulted away with first place, thanks to a tumbling-and-dance routine that struck Mandy as wholly unoriginal, but seemed to impress the judges. (The fact that the panel was made up entirely of teachers whom Mandy's skit made fun of might have had a little something to do with their decision, too.)

After the show, they'd found not just Jon, but Henley, Jen, and Megan waiting to congratulate them in the lobby.

"You guys were hilarious!" said Henley.

"Why, thank you," Evan said.

Allie passed out gum to everyone, while Henley slid up next to Mandy and whispered in her ear. "Are you guys . . ." She nodded just barely, but quite clearly, at Evan. ". . . you know, a couple?"

Mandy turned to her, eyes wide open. "No!" she said.

Instantly, every head turned in her direction.

She smiled meekly. "I mean, no thank you. No gum for me right now." Then she leaned over to Henley. "What I mean," she whispered back, "is that he's really, really nice. But we're really, *really* just friends."

Henley nodded and smiled just a little. "Cool," she said.

Mandy thought back on that moment as she sat at her computer. Could Henley *like* Evan? Wow! Seventh grade was full of surprises.

Then she sat back and read Allie's e-mail one more time. A movie sounded like fun, though she'd already talked with Kate about riding their bikes to the park.

There was a time when *Amanda* would have felt torn by this. But as she glanced up at the Latin motto taped to the wall above her desk, Mandy realized that those days were far behind her.

No doubt about it, if things kept going this way,

seventh grade was going to turn out to be the BEST YEAR EVER! Honestly. No lie.

Mandy sat up, grinned, and hit REPLY.

A movie sounds great. What time? I'm going to ride bikes with Kate at noon. Maybe we could all go after. I'll ask her. And maybe we could even ask Henley, and Evan, too.
YBFF,
Mandy
OBTW — I've been up for hours! :)

SEND.

About the Author

It's no secret that Lara Bergen has written many fabulous books, including the Candy Apple title *Drama Queen*. How she *ever* came up with a story about trying keeping secrets from your best friends, however, she'll never tell. Ever. Don't even ask her. A former editor, and cello player, she lives with her very real boyfriend (now her husband) in New York City . . . honest!

check out

TOTALLY CRUSHED

· BY Eliza Willard

Another

Candy Apple book . . .

just for you.

Phoebe was waiting for us in front of the school as promised, impatiently chomping on blueberry bubble gum.

"Sorry, Annabel. I can't let you into the building." She blocked me with her arm. "Spirit Week dress code violation. The blue coat has to go. No colors other than red and white allowed within fifty feet of Winchester Middle School property." She squinted at Sam's coat. "What color is that — rust?"

Sam looked down at his jacket. "Um, I guess you could call it rust. But it's in the red family."

"I'll let it slide this time," Phoebe said. "But you're on notice, bud."

I laughed. *She* was wearing blue jeans, black sneakers, and a green coat — not a speck of red that I could see. She's tall and has untamable blond curls that she'd bunched into a fat ponytail with a white elastic, but that elastic seemed awfully tiny to qualify for Red and White Day. "Where's *your* valentine outfit?" I asked.

"Ta da." She unzipped her coat. Underneath she wore a red superhero T-shirt with a big white *V* on it. "Victor to the rescue." Phoebe's younger brother, Victor, thinks he's a superhero called Kid Victorious. He's ten. Phoebe's parents tolerate this by letting him dress like a superhero most days. Phoebe thinks he should have grown out of it by now. We're afraid Victor is doomed to be a dweeb for life.

Sam grinned. "Now *that's* the Valentine's Day spirit."

"No, it isn't," I said. "The shirt just happens to be red. And it just happens to have the letter *V* on it. It has nothing to do with Valentine's Day. I'll let *you* slide this time," I teased Phoebe. "But you're on notice, girl."

She laughed.

The first bell rang, so we all went inside. "See you at lunchtime," Sam called, heading left toward his locker. Phoebe and I went the other way. Our lockers are next to each other since my last name (Lawson) comes right after hers (King) on the alphabetical class list. That's how we met last year, on the first day of sixth grade. I showed up on the first day of school and there she was, taping a poster of Spider-Man to the inside of her locker door. (She doesn't like to admit it, but the superhero fixation runs in the family.) She's over her Spider-Man phase now — she *says*. Sometimes I wonder.

We strolled down the eighth-grade hall. "Wow," I said. "Doesn't everything look great?"

The Spirit Week committee had decorated the school with hearts and balloons and red and white streamers. A big poster reminded everyone of the Carnation Code: white for teachers, pink for friends, red for crushes.

"Better than the usual toxic industrial green, that's for sure," Phoebe said.

Two popular eighth-graders, Josie Park and Theo Demopoulos, leaned against a locker, holding hands. In one arm Josie held a big heart-shaped candy box.

"It's their one-year anniversary," Phoebe said. "They started going out on Valentine's Day last year."

"I didn't know that," I said. "Seems like they've been together forever."

"Theo gave Josie a red carnation," Phoebe said. "Then he asked her to go to the skating party with him. And that was that. They've been together ever since."

"That's so romantic," I said.

"I know," Phoebe said. "Annabel, you're the heart expert. How do you think you know when you *really* like someone?"

I glanced at her, a little surprised. Usually *I* was the one with the gossip about who liked who and how they got together. Though I'd hardly call myself an expert. Phoebe suddenly seemed uncharacteristically interested in Valentine's Day. *And* she wouldn't meet my eye. Now I was suspicious.

"Well," I said. "I think I've got it figured out. When you really like someone, there are signs. The first one is butterflies in your stomach, worse than on a test day. Then you get goose bumps on your forearms. Finally, you get a spacy, head-spinning feeling I call Crush Dizziness."

"Have you ever felt the signs?" Phoebe asked.

"Two out of three," I said. "But since I had a stomach flu at the time, the butterflies might not have been from a crush."

"But how do you know?" Phoebe asked. "You've never had a real boyfriend."

"That's true," I said. "But I've seen a lot of movies, listened to a lot of songs, and read a lot of books."

"Still," she said.

As usual, Phoebe was right. I've liked plenty of boys, but so far none of them had returned the favor. I even had a few so-called "boyfriends" in elementary school — boys who sat with me at lunch or invited me to their birthday parties, only to stop as soon as some other boy started teasing them about being a "cootie-coated girl-toucher," or some other inventive nickname. Then the boys would all run off to poke at a dead frog they found. Like rotting amphibian corpses aren't loaded with cooties. My point being: A boy who dumps you for a dead frog doesn't count as a real boyfriend.

Across the hall, Josie opened her giant box of candy and fed Theo a chocolate. I sighed. To think it all started with a red carnation.

"Wouldn't it be great if something like that happened to *us* this year?" I said. "If we got red carnations, and someone asked us to the skating party?"

"*Really* great," Phoebe said.

"You like someone," I said.

"No, I don't," she said.

"Yes, you do," I said. "Phoebe, it's so obvious."

She pulled her head out of her locker and finally looked at me. Her face was magenta.

This was big. The weird thing was, I couldn't imagine who in the world she could possibly like. I had absolutely no idea. And we were supposed to be best friends.

"Who?" I said. "Who is it? Phoebs, I'm your best friend. If you can't tell me, who can you tell?"

"In a way you're the worst person in the world to tell," she said.

"Why?" I said.

"Because — you know him."

"Know who? Who are you talking about?"

"All right," she said. "I'll tell you. But you have to promise not to laugh."

"I promise," I said. "Tell me before my head explodes."

"Okay," she said. "I like . . . Sam."

"Sam?!?" At first the name did not compute. *Sam? Sam who?* "You mean, Sam Arkin? My next-door neighbor Sam?"

She nodded. She looked so embarrassed I could tell this was a heavy crush. Like, really serious. Still, I found it hard to believe.

"You like Sam Arkin," I said one more time, for confirmation.

"Yes," she said.

"You," I repeated, pointing right at her so it would be perfectly clear which *you* I was talking about, "like *Sam —*"

"Stop it, Annabel. Yes, me. I like Sam."

"For how long?" I asked. "How long could you keep a secret like this from me?"

"I don't really know," she said. "I just looked at him one day last week and it hit me. I like him."

"That's so great!" I squealed. I was beginning to realize what this meant. My best friend liked my other best friend. Fantastic! My two favorite people in the world — as a couple! What could be better? Or more efficient? Phoebe could have a boyfriend, and Sam could have a girlfriend, and my life wouldn't have to change at all.

After Spanish, then gym, then the longest math class in academic history (*If x = 1 carnation,* Mr. Mackey, our teacher, said, *and y = no carnations, how do we solve this problem?*), the lunch bell finally rang. I shot out of algebra like a spitball through a straw. Students flooded the halls, laughing and squealing. The lockers looked like floats in the Rose Bowl parade, covered with pink and red flowers. Mostly pink, but there was enough red on display to give a girl hope.

I rounded the corner and dashed to my locker. Phoebe hadn't arrived yet. I saw her locker first — a sea of pink. No red. Rats.

Then I saw mine. *Yes!* I got five pink carnations — and a red one!

This was it! Who could it be from?

My fingers trembled as I pulled the red flower

off my locker. The pink ones could wait. A tag was wrapped around the stem. I turned it over.

It said, "From Sam Arkin."

I read it again, just to be sure there was no mistake.

"From Sam Arkin."

That had to be wrong. Better read it again.

"From Sam Arkin."

No. *From Sam Arkin?* No!!!!

"From Sam Arkin."

This couldn't be.

My heart stopped. *Sam? The girl he likes is . . . me?*

Phoebe bounded toward me down the hall, almost flying in her Kid Victorious T-shirt, eager as a puppy to see if she'd gotten any flowers. *Phoebe . . .* What was I going to do? This would break her heart. I couldn't let her know, not yet. I tossed the red carnation into a dark corner of my locker and flashed her my biggest, fakest smile, which made me feel like I was impersonating Ari Berg. Not a good feeling. So much for me being the best friend ever.

"What'd we get? What'd we get?" Phoebe asked as she scanned her locker. Her face fell. "Nothing but pink. Oh, well. Did you get a red one, Annabel?"

I shook my head. "All pink, too." I tore a pink

flower off and read the tag. It was from Phoebe. "Hey! Thanks, Phoebs."

She waved the pink carnation I'd sent her. "Thanks to you, too. And look — here's one from Sam." Sam had sent her a pink carnation. Because they were friends. Just friends.

I could tell Phoebe was a little disappointed, but she's a good sport and she tried to hide it. One of her down-to-earth qualities is the ability to accept reality without too much whining. My mother mentions how much she admires that quality every time we have liver for dinner. Liver is disgusting and I'm not afraid to express my feelings about it by whining. Phoebe would just smile and choke it down.

The crowd in the hall began to thin as people headed for lunch. Sam rounded the corner and made a beeline for us, a big smile on his face. Oh, no!

He was expecting a big happy smile from me, no doubt. A thrilled thank you, and maybe even a hug. Gack!

The hug was not happening. Not with Phoebe standing right there. Or under any other circumstances.

Phoebe saw him and lit up. Sam was sure to say something about the flowers — and Phoebe would be heartbroken. I couldn't let that happen. I needed some time to straighten out this mess.

"Hey!" Sam said. "How did you —"

"Lunchtime!" I said. "Gotta go!" I grabbed Phoebe's arm and dragged her away toward the cafeteria before Sam had a chance to finish his Sentence of Doom.

"Annabel! What are you doing?" Phoebe tried to free herself from my kung-fu grip, but I wasn't letting go. I could tell she was annoyed with me. I didn't care. "Why didn't you give me a chance to talk to Sam? He might have asked me to the skating party!"

"Sorry," I said. "I'm just so hungry! I'm dying for some —" We'd reached the cafeteria. The menu was posted on the door. I scanned it in search of inspiration. "Brussels sprouts! Yes, Brussels sprouts. Gotta have some."

We were safely inside the cafeteria door. I let her go. She rubbed her wrist and glared at me. "Brussels sprouts?" she said. "Since when — ?"

"Great source of vitamin C," I said, dragging her to the food line and hoping I was somewhat right.

"If it's vitamin C you want, a glass of orange juice will take care of it," Phoebe said, tugging her arm away.

I barely listened. I had bigger problems. Like finding a way to keep from breaking the hearts of my two best friends.

check out

CALLIE FOR PRESIDENT

BY ROBIN WASSERMAN

another

CANDY APPLE book . . .

just for you.

"Are you crazy?" I whispered, leaning across the aisle toward Fish's desk.

He stared straight ahead. But he couldn't fool me. Fish had never in his life paid attention in social studies class, and I was pretty sure he wasn't starting any time soon.

"Fish!" I hissed. "*Fish!* How can you agree to work on Brianna's campaign?"

"Shhh!" Fish finally turned toward me, crossed his eyes, stuck out his tongue, then whipped his head back around to the front of the class. I sighed. Fish could never take anything seriously. Not even something like *this*.

Max, who sat behind me, tapped me on the shoulder. She tipped her glittery orange pen toward Mr. Hamilton, who was trying — and failing — to explain us why anyone would ever want to run for class secretary. Mr. Hamilton was the faculty sponsor for the seventh grade class council, which meant he had to pretend he cared. The rest of us didn't.

"Definitely a new shirt," Max whispered. "I give it a six." I shook my head, and held up four fingers, biting down on the corners of my lips so I wouldn't laugh.

Here's the thing about Mr. Hamilton. He may be a teacher, and he may be kind of old (though not as old as, like, my dad) but he doesn't act like it. He wears green Converse sneakers that are almost as beat up as my pink ones — only his aren't duct-taped together. His hair is always sticking straight up, and rumor is, he plays bass guitar in a band on the weekends.

Basically, he's cool.

And I don't mean cool like Brianna Blake and her posse. Because they're not cool, they're popular. Trust me, there's a difference.

He's cool like some indie punk rocker who's too cool to be on the radio, cool like he should be working in a coffee shop in New York City and writing poetry on the side — way too cool for Susan B. Anthony Middle School. But the weird thing is, he acts like he wants to be here. He acts like he actually likes teaching, and seventh graders, and social studies. He gets all excited about whatever he's teaching us, and no matter how boring we think it's going to be, he gets us excited, too.

Which may be the coolest thing of all.

Mr. Hamilton wears a different t-shirt every day, usually with the name of some band no one's ever heard of. Some of them are sort-of-cool, some of them are tres-cool, and some of them are ultra-cool. (That day's shirt was grey with black lettering across the front reading: *Soul Asylum,* whatever that meant.) Max and I developed a rating system. It kept us awake during the very rare moments when Mr. Hamilton was being kind of boring.

Like now.

"And of course, the class council president will be in charge of planning the year's big fundraising event, which is traditionally a winter carnival," Mr. Hamilton droned. You got the feeling that even *he* was bored. "And at the end of the year, the president will work with the rest of the council to decide how the money will be spent."

Max snorted. I knew what she was thinking. Mr. Hamilton made it sound like some big mystery. But we all knew how the money would be spent. Just like every other year, Brianna Blake would run, Brianna Blake would win, then Brianna Blake and her buddies would raise money with a winter carnival and spend it all on a big spring dance. A spring dance that nobody but Brianna Blake and her buddies wanted to go to. Who wants to spend a Saturday night standing around the gym, drinking raspberry punch and breathing in the stench of sweat socks?

I'll tell you who: Brianna Blake.

She was sitting front and center, same as she does in every class, staring up at Mr. Hamilton like every word out of his mouth was the most amazing sound she'd ever heard. Her seat gave her a much better view of Mr. Hamilton's t-shirt collection, but my seat way in the back gave me the chance to ball up tiny pieces of paper and flick them at Fish's head, trying to force him to turn around. It didn't work.

"And now, drumroll please . . . I'll open up the nominations for class council president!" Mr. Hamilton announced dramatically. Just when you thought Mr. Hamilton was different from all the rest of the teachers, he'd say something kind of cheesy to remind you that he belonged here after all. But I forgave him. Even cool people have to be uncool once in a while; it makes them even cooler. "Who would like to —"

"I nominate Brianna Blake?" Britney shouted, jumping out of her seat and waving her hand in the air.

Brianna smiled and looked down at her desk, like she was embarrassed. But I knew it was just an act.

Mr. Hamilton nodded. "Okay, does anyone second the —"

"I second the nomination!" Ashton shrieked. She flashed Brianna a grin and a thumbs up. Brianna ignored her. She fixed her laser stare on Mr. Hamilton instead, and gave him her most dazzling smile.

"I'd be honored to be a candidate," she said sweetly, smoothing down her blond hair — not that it ever needed smoothing. "It's such a privilege to be able to serve my school . . . I mean, if I win, of course."

Of course.

Mr. Hamilton didn't smile back.

I decided to up that day's t-shirt rating to a ten. Extra points for good behavior.

"Okay, so we have Brianna running," he said. "Anyone else?"

Silence.

Everyone knew that Brianna Blake wanted to be class council president, and everyone knew that what Brianna Blake wanted, Brianna Blake got.

Mr. Hamilton cleared his throat. "I'm sure *someone* wants to run. An election is a great way to engage your civic consciousness — and we can't have a real campaign with only one candidate, now can we?"

"See?" I whispered to Fish. "It's not even a real campaign, so I don't know why you have to work on it."

Fish twisted around. "Maybe I *want* to," he whispered back.

"You're going to have to suck up to her like all the rest of them," Max muttered.

Fish wiggled his eyebrows and gave us an evil grin. "What if I make *her* suck up to me instead? Ever think of that?"

I rolled my eyes. Fish didn't get it. Once he got dragged into Brianna Blake's evil vortex of shallowness, there'd be no escape. She was like a black hole of blond. "Why don't you just tell her you changed your —"

"Callie?" Mr. Hamilton said, waving at me. "I hate to interrupt your very important conversation, but we're kind of in the middle of something up here."

I could feel my face turning tomato red. "Oh, uh, sorry, Mr. Hamilton. I, uh . . . sorry."

He raised his eyebrows. "Care to share your thoughts with the rest of the class?"

"I . . . um . . ." I took a deep breath. "I don't have any thoughts right now, Mr. Hamilton."

The whole class started laughing, even Max and Fish.

"How about you, Max?" Mr. Hamilton asked. Max's giggles morphed into a cough. "You've *always* got something to say."

"Oh, uh, we were, uh, just —"

"Maybe you were about to express your civic duty by throwing your hat into the ring?" he asked.

"My — what?" Max wrinkled her forehead.

Mr. Hamilton gave her an encouraging smile. "The topic of today's discussion is the race for class council president," he reminded her. "And it occurs to me that, given your interest in history and politics, perhaps you'd like to —"

"I nominate Callie!" Max yelped.

I almost jumped out of my seat. *"What?"* I whirled around to glare at her. She shrugged, and mouthed *sorry*. But that wasn't going to cut it.

"Callie Singer?" I heard someone mutter — it sounded like Britney. "You've got to be kidding?"

Fish's hand shot into the air. "I second the nomination!" he shouted, loud and clear.

For the second time that day, I closed my eyes and wished that I was in the middle of a dream.

For the second time that day, my wish didn't come true. And when I opened my eyes, Mr. Hamilton's *Soul Asylum* t-shirt was staring me in the face.

"Congratulations, Callie," he said, as I glared at Fish and Max, wishing for laser-powered eyes that could burn holes right through my former best friends' foreheads. "Looks like you're running for president."

"How *could* you?" I cried, as soon as we escaped from the classroom.

"Problem, Madame President?" Fish asked innocently.

"What were you thinking?" I shook Max by the shoulders. "Are you trying to torture me?"

Max wriggled out of my grasp. "You're the one who's always whining about how Brianna Blake wins everything," she pointed out, pushing her glasses up on her nose. "Now's your chance to beat her."

"Beat her?" I asked, my eyes widening. "*Beat her*? Didn't you hear everyone in there —" I winced — "laughing at me? They know I can't beat Brianna. Nobody can. But you two, my supposed best friends . . . ." It's hard to talk when your heart is thumping in your chest and your brain is stuffed full of one thought repeated a million times: *What am I going to do now? What am I going to do now? WhatamIgoingtodonow . . . ?*

So whatever came out of me next — half squeak, half growl — wasn't quite in English. But it got the point across. I turned my back on the two of them and started speed-walking to the cafeteria. I needed a serious sugar rush to wash the last hour out of my system.

But it's harder to get rid of best friends than bad memories. They followed me.

"I'm sorry," Max said, tugging at my shoulder. "I just blurted it out before I knew what I was saying. I didn't mean to."

"Well I did," Fish said indignantly. "You'd make a great president, Callie. And you're always saying that someone should run against Brianna. Why not you?"

"You *would* be good," Max said hesitantly. "And you have plenty of opinions about how to run things."

"Yeah, you're always bossing *us* around," Fish pointed out.

Max gave him a light shove. "We're supposed to be apologizing," she reminded him a stage whisper. "Save the insults for *after* she forgives us."

I rolled my eyes. "You know *she's* standing right here, right? And you're definitely not forgiven yet."

I stopped at my locker to ditch my books before lunch. Max leaned back against the metal doors, her eyes glowing. "Think about the possibilities," she said. "You're always complaining how the class council never does anything for people like us, right?"

"The class council doesn't know that people like us exist," I grumbled.

"And you love bossing people around," Fish added. He'd said that before.

I gave him a light shove. "I love bossing *you* around," I teased.

"How many times a day do you start a sentence with 'If I were in charge around here'?" Max asked.

"Once a week," I said. "Maybe."

Fish snorted. "Try ten times a day. *At least.*"

"This could be our chance — I mean, your chance," Max continued. "To tell the school what you *really* think. And make them realize that just because Brianna's blond and beautiful —"

"Not that beautiful," I said.

"Just because people *think* she's blond and beautiful —"

"Well, she really *is* blond," Fish pointed out. "I don't think you can call that a matter of opinion."

Max slammed her palm flat against the locker. "It's not just about Brianna Blake!" she sputtered. "It's about taking a stand against all the lame stuff that this school throws at us every day. We could actually change the way things are done. We could actually —"

"Make a difference?" I guessed, only half-teasing. Sure, it sounded cheesy and after-school-special-y. But it also sounded kind of good. Max and Fish were right. I *did* have a lot to say. And there were plenty of things I would change about Susan B. Anthony Middle School, if I got the chance.

But, I suddenly realized, that was a pretty big *if.*